ALSO BY LESLEY M. M. BLUME

Cornelia and the Audacious Escapades of the Somerset Sisters

Modern Fairies, Dwarves, Goblins, and Other Nasties:
A Practical Guide by Miss Edythe McFate

The Rising Star of Rusty Nail

Tennyson

The Wondrous Journals of Dr. Wendell Wellington Wiggins

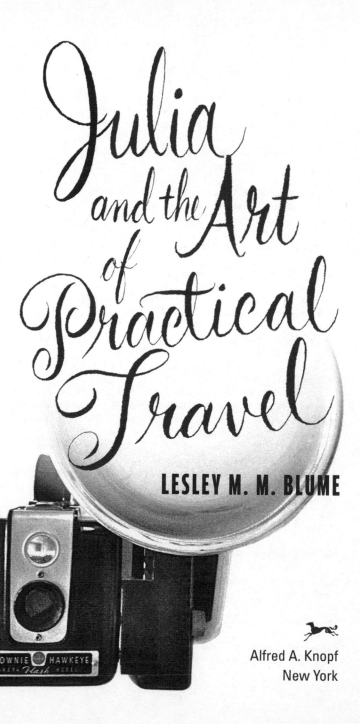

Julia and the Art of Practical Travel

LESLEY M. M. BLUME

Alfred A. Knopf
New York

THIS IS A BORZOI BOOK PUBLISHED BY ALFRED A. KNOPF

Visit us on the Web! randomhousekids.com

Educators and librarians, for a variety of teaching tools, visit us at RHTeachersLibrarians.com

Library of Congress Cataloging-in-Publication Data
Blume, Lesley M. M.
Julia and the art of practical travel / Lesley M.M. Blume.—First edition.
pages cm
Summary: In 1968, eleven-year-old Julia and her Aunt Constance are forced to sell their family home, Windy Ridge, in New York's Hudson Valley and embark on a cross-country automobile trip in search of Julia's mother, bringing only three travel trunks and some outlandish "practical travel things."
ISBN 978-0-385-75282-4 (trade) — ISBN 978-0-385-75283-1 (lib. bdg.) — ISBN 978-0-385-75284-8 (ebook)
[1. Automobile travel—Fiction. 2. Aunts—Fiction. 3. Missing persons—Fiction. 4. United States—History—1961–1969—Fiction.] I. Title.
PZ7.B62567Jul 2015
[Fic]—dc23
213044490

The text of this book is set in 13-point Garamond.

Printed in the United States of America
March 2015
10 9 8 7 6 5 4 3 2 1
First Edition

For Glynnis,
the patron saint of practical-yet-lavish travel

CONTENTS

PART ONE

New York

CHAPTER ONE

Windy Ridge

That's the problem with living in a small town: everyone knows everyone else. So when Belfry and I went to the five-and-dime and told Mr. Jeffreys that we wanted to buy a packet of cigarettes, he told us that we were too young and he wouldn't sell them to us. Belfry told him, No, we're not too young, we're sixteen, and Mr. Jeffreys snorted and said, Like fun you are. You, Belfry, are twelve, he went on, and you, Julia, are only eleven, and don't try to fool me, because I've known you both since you were in diapers. Then he gave us a packet of Beemans gum and told us, Good try, be good, and we trudged outside again.

I don't know why you wanted them so much anyway, I told Belfry and added that Mr. Hopper, who delivered the groceries, smoked cigarettes, and his hands and breath always smelled like a stinky old basement. Belfry sighed and told me that all grown-ups in movies smoked and that you might as well wear a diaper if you didn't.

And now we don't have any other choice, he added as we walked back to my house. I asked him what he meant, and he pulled up a handful of clover from the side of the road and started sucking the nectar out from the buds.

We're just going to have to grow our own tobacco, he said.

How are we going to do that? I asked him. Everyone knows that you have to be given seeds from the Indians and then grow them in a big field in South Carolina. It's 1968, I reminded him, and there haven't been Indians here in the Hudson Valley for a million years.

But Belfry, who never gives up on anything, said that he had a plan, and the very next day he sent away for a catalog and about four weeks after that, the tobacco seeds arrived in a brown paper box tied up with twine.

Now, Belfry said, we have to grow these at your house, because if we grow them at mine, my old man will find them and take them for himself. And I read that you have to grow the seeds in real china cups and we don't have any at home, and your grandma has tons, he told me.

I had never heard this before but knew better than to question Belfry, who reads every magazine in the stand at the grocery store and knows more than me about everything in the world. And it was true about the teacups; we had about a thousand of them lying around in splintery crates that had words like *fragile* and *holiday* and *heirloom* written on the side boards.

So that's what we were doing when Aunt Constance walked in that day, the day that my life at Windy Ridge ended and my life everyplace else began: planting the seeds from the brown box in Grandmother's teacups out in the gardening shed, in a spot where the sun shines through the window all day, so it would be hot and bright like it must be in South Carolina.

Julia, said Aunt Constance as she pushed the door open. What are you doing in here? And then her eyes got really wide and she said, What on earth are you doing with your grandmother's best bone china?

Is it really made from bones? asked Belfry.

No, it's not, but it's very expensive anyway, said Aunt Constance, and then because she's always very polite, she said, Hello, Belfry, and then she peered into the cups. Why have you filled our family's best heirloom china with dirt? she asked.

When Belfry told her that we were planting strawberries, Aunt Constance smiled and her shoulders relaxed and she said it was a lovely idea, but that we should have asked before using the cups. Didn't we know, she said, that this china was a wedding present when Great-great-grandmother Lancaster married Lord Ashley, and that the crown prince of England had been at the ceremony, and that there was very little of the china left after all that time had passed?

No, said Belfry, I hadn't known that, and I just kept quiet, because I actually had known that, and I'd taken the china cups anyway. Here is a picture of one that I took with my Brownie camera, which I carry with me at all times:

Then Aunt Constance got a very grave look on her face.

Julia, she said, I need you to come with me. Your grandmother would like to speak with you.

Belfry wasn't allowed to come along, but Aunt Constance let him bring home a bone china cup filled with tobacco seeds and dirt because she felt rude about not including him.

See you tomorrow, he said, winking at me as he stalked away with the cup in his hands.

Yeah, see you then, I said, with my heart in my throat. Nothing good ever came from being called upstairs to have a talk with Grandmother.

If you live in our town, you know our house, Windy Ridge, already. If you live anywhere in the county, you probably know it, and maybe even if you live in New York City, way down the Hudson River. It's a famous house and a big one, made from gray stones that were dug up out from the Windy Ridge ground a long time ago, and there are lots of tall trees that bend and whisper at night and sometimes get struck by lightning in the summer storms.

The Lancasters—my family—have lived at Windy Ridge forever and my great-great-grandmother Lancaster, who got given the bone teacups at her wedding, once let George Washington live here for a while when we were fighting England. Belfry says that George Washington had wooden teeth, which sounds pretty awful and splintery, if you ask me. One time, in the garden, we found a piece of wood that looked like a tooth. I was sure it had been one of George Washington's teeth. Belfry said, No, don't be stupid: wood rots; there's no way one of George Washington's teeth would have lasted this long. But I kept it anyway and put it inside my silver treasure box, in between some periwinkle sea glass I found on the beach in Newport and my mother's pink pearl necklace that she threw in a bush once, after Grandmother made her go to a stuffy party. Grandmother never could get the dirt off the strings between the pearls, and that's why she gave it to me.

I followed Aunt Constance across the lawns and past the walled garden, which was covered with thorny wild yellow roses. It was a hot day, even for August, and Aunt Constance's neck looked sweaty as she walked in front of me. She always wore her faded red hair in a bun on the top of her head. It was cool inside the house because thick old stone walls don't let in heat, even when all of the windows are open. The tall clock in the hallway rumbled with chimes as we walked past it.

Grandmother's room was right at the top of the stairs, so she could see who was going up and down and know everything that's going on. She used to come downstairs to be served breakfast and take her walk in the gardens. And she would come downstairs later in the day for tea-time, and then again for supper, of course wearing different clothes each time. Our housekeeper, Winifred, used to serve Grandmother the breakfasts, teas, and sup-

pers, but she had to get let go a few years ago, and then
Aunt Constance did it instead. But lately Grandmother
hadn't been coming downstairs for any of these things.
She just stayed in her huge oak canopy bed and asked for
her jewelry box and put different old rings on her long
fingers.

Today she was wearing her big fire-opal ring that had a
bunch of diamonds around it, which to me always looked
like stones around a campfire:

Sit down and stop taking photographs with that thing,
Julia, Aunt Constance told me in her powdery voice. In
fact, give it to me, she added.

I put the camera on the floor instead of giving it to her. I never liked anyone else to touch my camera; I even slept with it next to my bed at night. My mother gave it to me for my seventh birthday and it was the last present she ever gave to me. Aunt Constance's forehead crinkled into a frown when I disobeyed her, but she didn't ask for the camera again. Instead she took a deep breath and said:

Grandmother has something to tell you.

What is it, Grandmother? I asked, sitting in a chair next to her bed.

Grandmother looked at me very hard, and after a minute, she said: Jooooolia (she always made my name sound like it had a hundred letters in it). And I said, Yes? And then she said something that I will never forget if I live to be a thousand years old.

Joooooolia, Grandmother said. I have decided that by noon tomorrow, I will be dead.

I didn't know what to say. I knew that I was supposed to find the polite thing to say, because manners are very important to Grandmother. So after a minute, I replied: I am very sorry to hear that. And then I added, Why have you decided this?

Grandmother looked very grave. Because I have outlived my times, she told me.

Aunt Constance moved around in her chair and started to say, That's not true, Mother—but Grandmother raised her hand and Aunt Constance stopped talking right away. Words always dry up in the air when Grandmother raises her hand, especially when she's wearing the fire-opal ring.

From now on, you shall have to take care of each other, she told us, and went on: I suspect, Constance, that you will have to sell Windy Ridge and all of its contents.

I didn't say anything, because I knew that Grandmother was joking and you shouldn't interrupt someone when they're telling a joke, even a not-funny one. As I've said, the Lancasters have lived at Windy Ridge for hundreds of years. But Aunt Constance seemed to be missing the joke. She looked like someone had sucked the breath right out of her body.

Will that be necessary? she asked when she could talk again.

I'm afraid so, said Grandmother. Unfortunately, the Lancasters haven't been particularly financially prudent in recent generations, she added.

I didn't know what this meant and it sounded a bit boring, so I tuned out this part of the conversation until Grandmother said something that caught my attention:

And I think it's time to send Jooooooolia to Miss Horton's. I'm certain that they will accept her when she turns twelve—and on scholarship too—just to have a Lancaster there again.

Now I thought that Grandmother was taking the joke a little bit too far. Miss Horton's was a snobby boarding school for teenage girls from good families. She had gone there and so had Aunt Constance and my mother too, until she got kicked out for being a bad influence on the other girls.

And then I suddenly remembered something: Grandmother actually never tells jokes and thinks that jokes are vulgar. I started to feel how you feel on a summer day when you've just gotten out of a pool and a cloud comes out of nowhere and covers up the sun. You've gone from being warm and happy to shivery and damp, and have to huddle up with your arms around your knees until the sun comes back out.

All right, Mother, said Aunt Constance slowly. If that's what you think is best.

No one ever says no to Grandmother.

Joooooolia, said Grandmother.

Yes? I said.

It would be a grave disappointment to me if you turned out like your mother, wherever she may be at this moment, she said.

But after noon tomorrow, you'll be gone, I pointed out. So how can you be disappointed?

Grandmother glared at me. You will *always* know when I'm disappointed, no matter where I am, she told me. Now run along. Constance, stay with me.

So I picked up my camera, left the room, and did what any girl in her right mind would do: I left the door

open just a crack and eavesdropped. I wanted to know
if Grandmother really intended to die by noon, and
whether they really were going to sell Windy Ridge and
send me off to Miss Horton's. But Aunt Constance was
on to me: she came and shut the door firmly, and she
and Grandmother kept talking in their discreet church
voices. I gave up then and walked downstairs and tried
to imagine what the world looked like when you didn't
live at Windy Ridge. I wanted to take pictures of every
single thing in the house because it was all starting to
fade in front of my very eyes, and I worried that it all
might just disappear completely before the sun rose
again. Things were always disappearing from Windy
Ridge. Like my mother, for example. So if you wanted
to remember anything clearly, you had to take a picture
of it quick.

But it was too dark by then; all of the pictures would
have come out black and it would be a waste of film,
which costs a lot of money, so I just ambled around with
a funny, hollow feeling in my stomach. I ran my hands
over the cool marble walk-in dining-hall fireplaces, and
ran up and down the splintery secret staircase at the back
of the house, and finally went outside and sat next to the
dovecote, which had pale, dirty white paint peeling off
the sides. I listened to the doves cooing their sad twilight
songs and stared at Grandmother's window. The yellow
light stayed on all night behind the drawn lace curtains,

until it went out at around five in the morning, just before dawn.

When Aunt Constance came to find me a little while
later, she was wearing a black dress, so I knew that Grandmother was gone.

Lancasters always keep their word.

CHAPTER TWO

The Grand Sale

It rained on the day of Grandmother's funeral, but practically the whole town came to the church anyway. And after telling Aunt Constance and me how sorry they were about the tragic news and how Grandmother had been a pillar of the community, some of the women said in very low voices to Aunt Constance that they'd heard an intriguing rumor that we were going to have a house sale—did this happen to be true? And then when Aunt Constance said that yes, it was true; we were planning on selling Windy Ridge and all of its contents, those women looked very excited and not at all funeral-sad and promised that they'd be there, bright and early.

The day before the sale, I helped Aunt Constance tie price tags around all of our furniture. At first I took pictures of everything, but she told me that I'd better stop: it was going to be harder for us to get an endless supply of film so easily in the future. And then she got upset when I taped tags right onto the family portraits in the dining room and parlors. Didn't I know, she said, that these were Gainsboroughs, for goodness' sake?

I still didn't understand why we were taping tags onto everything in the first place, so I asked her, Aunt Constance, why are we selling all of our family paintings that famous painters made and getting rid of all of our family's things that famous people gave us—is it because we need the money? Is that why I won't be able to get more film too? I informed her that I absolutely needed to have film with me at all times.

Aunt Constance's face turned as red as her hair, and she said that it wasn't nice for young ladies to discuss financial matters, and I never did get my answers.

But later, when she was in the mood to talk again, I asked her: When we sell Windy Ridge, where are we going to live? Am I going to have to go to Miss Horton's to learn how to sit up flagpole straight and walk with a book on my head?

Aunt Constance sat down on a wicker couch that made sort of a crunching noise whenever you moved around on it. You are not going to Miss Horton's right away, she told me. They won't admit you until later this year, when you turn twelve. In the meantime, I have to go on a car trip, and you'll have to come with me.

Where are we going? I asked, hoping for the beach at Newport. It was still very hot out and we hadn't been anywhere that summer, and we never swam in the Hudson River. Every summer somebody went in and got caught in the currents and drowned. Not even Belfry would jump in, and he was brave enough to eat live bees when he was showing off for someone.

Come sit next to me, said Aunt Constance, and the wicker couch made an extra-crunchy noise when I plopped down next to her. Aunt Constance looked very grave.

We are going to find your mother, she told me.

Oh, I said, and then the cloud-over-the-sun feeling came back. And my heart started to beat a little faster, like it does when you drink tea with too much sugar in it. After a moment, I added: But I thought no one knows where she is.

We don't, Aunt Constance said, but now we have to find her. There is Lancaster business to be addressed. She needs to be told about Grandmother's passing. Half of the proceeds from the house sale will belong to her. And if we cannot find her, those proceeds will belong to you instead.

When I asked what proceeds were, Aunt Constance shuddered and said: Money. Then she told me to follow her up to the attic, where she'd set aside three big travel trunks, a silver tea set, a big case of silver tableware, a set of china, a cuckoo clock, a wind-up phonograph player, and a bunch of other practical-travel things that she said we'd need for our trip:

We would leave, she said, the moment that someone bought Windy Ridge.

Once, while we were playing cards, I asked Grandmother what was so bad about my mother.

We raised her beautifully, but she turned into a dirty hippie, said Grandmother. Then she yelled, *Gin!* and laid down her cards on the table: she'd won the hand with a straight of spades.

Later that day, I asked Belfry what a dirty hippie was. He told me that hippies wore flowers in their hair and said things like "groovy" and smoked cigarettes made from green tobacco called grass. I didn't think that sounded so terrible and wondered why Grandmother hated hippies so much. The only other things she'd hated that much: Communists (whatever they were), bad manners, and that skunk that once crawled under Windy Ridge's back porch and died.

My mother has been gone for a long time. Or anyway, since I was eight, which is three whole years ago. She used to live with us at Windy Ridge, where she grew up like all proper Lancasters, but she never liked teatime or playing cards or walking in the gardens with Aunt Constance and Grandmother. Instead she liked sitting alone on the house's roof and staring at the stars all night and listening to records in her room. She let her hair get long and tangly, like a wild horse's tail. Sometimes she slept out down by the riverbank. She stopped going into town because people talked about her in stage whispers and stared at her rudely. They talked about me in stage whispers too and said things like my mother never wanted a baby in the first place, and one woman even said once that my mother used to pretend that I wasn't her daughter at all, just a distant Lancaster cousin who happened to get dropped off at Windy Ridge one day even though we looked just the same and everyone knew that I was hers.

And one morning my mother was gone, and if there was a note, I was never told about it.

After my mother went away, Grandmother was suddenly very tired all the time. Before then I had to do all of the Lancaster things that my mother had been taught about too and hated, but once Grandmother had gotten tired, she stopped watching me all the time and making me learn about gardening and elocution and how to introduce people properly to one another. My governess disappeared too—she was let go along with Winifred, our housekeeper, Aunt Constance explained one morning—but she and Grandmother somehow forgot to enroll me in a regular school instead, and by the time they realized they'd forgotten, it was so late in the year that they decided I should just wait and start school next year. And no one said anything about me and Belfry hanging around together, even though before Grandmother got tired she would have sent him packing with one glare. I was very glad to have Belfry, who would always help his dad rake our lawns in the fall and mow the grass in the summer. Belfry never whispered about my mother or the fact that she didn't even know who my father was and that I'd never been to a real school.

When there were just three of us left—me, Grandmother, and Aunt Constance—the house felt very echoey and empty. Every night before I went to sleep, I went into my mother's room and sat at her vanity table and combed my hair with her shiny black Mason Pearson brush:

We have the same color hair, my mother and I. And I wondered how long her hair was now and whether she thought about me at all, and when I got too sad, I made myself leave the room and not think about her anymore. It was hard not to think about her all the time after she first left Windy Ridge, even though most of the time she'd pretended that I wasn't there and I wasn't hers. But it was still hard, and there was an empty space shaped like her in the house, so I had to train myself to think about other things besides that empty space. Soon I got better at it.

As my governess used to say: Practice makes perfect.

• • •

The day of the house sale arrived, and people covered every inch of our house like locusts. They asked me lots of pesty questions about why we were selling Windy Ridge, and I didn't want to talk to them so I went under the front porch, which was the only place where you could escape and not be seen. It was cool there too. Belfry came to the house and knew where to find me, of course, and the floorboards over our heads creaked and sighed as the townspeople went in and out of Windy Ridge, carrying armfuls of our Lancaster things back to their station wagons.

Just then a silver car turned up the long, winding road that led up to our house; it glinted in the sun as it followed the driveway's curve left and right and then left again. It was the biggest car I'd ever seen, a shining silver monster growling up the road, and when it stopped in front of the porch, a woman popped out and suddenly the air was choked up with her perfume. She marched up the stairs like a queen coming home, and Belfry and I heard her holler out:

Constance Lancaster! It has been simply years. What— don't you remember me? It's Tipsy, darling! Tipsy von Lipp.

Aunt Constance, who'd been standing in the foyer, must have given her a blank stare, for this woman then said in a lower voice this time:

You know, Shirley Hicks. From church—remember? But now I go by Tipsy, darling!

Oh yes, said Aunt Constance slowly. How are you after all these years, Shirley?

Never better, said the woman, and added: Three husbands later, I'm rich as Onassis. And when I heard that Windy Ridge was for sale, I came up right away to buy it—lock, stock, and barrel. I want everything, darling—absolutely everything!

Oh Lord, what a beast, said Belfry under his breath.

Well, from under the porch we could hear pretty much all that happened next: Aunt Constance laughed sort of nervously and said, Please have a look around; there are lots of lovely items to choose from. Then Tipsy Hicks said that no, she meant it, she wanted to buy everything, name your price. So Aunt Constance, who hates talking about money more than anything, said she couldn't possibly name a price for everything, and then Shirley Hicks said, Here is a blank check; you can even fill it in yourself if you like. And all of the ladies who'd been lurking around and eavesdropping in the bushes and rooms nearby gasped. Belfry and I heard one lady standing near the porch say under her breath to another lady:

That Shirley Hicks has probably been waiting her whole life for this moment, when she could sail back into town rich after her poor childhood and then buy up the biggest place in town.

Well, said the other lady, putting on a crown doesn't make you a queen, you know.

I sat there quietly under the porch as the Tipsy woman scratched out a check to Aunt Constance, and wondered why these sorts of things were so important to grown-ups.

Maybe they teach you to be that way at places like Miss Horton's.

Later that night, after Tipsy Lipps bought our home, where Lancasters had lived for hundreds of years, and everything in it besides our practical-travel things in the attic, Aunt Constance told me that we would leave on our trip the very next day. We would start our search for my mother, she said, in New York City. She and Grandmother had heard a rumor that my mother had gone off to find other hippies in the Village, so that's where we'd start looking for her, said Aunt Constance.

But I thought we were going to the city, not a village, I said.

The Village is a neighborhood in the city, Aunt Constance told me. Artists live there—lots of them. Poets, painters—even fiddlers, probably.

And hippies, of course, she added.

I asked if Belfry could come too, that he seemed to know a lot about hippies and might be useful to us, but

Aunt Constance said that no, this was a private family matter. I was to pull together my clothes and remaining possessions, which she would put in one of the travel trunks. So I gave her my photograph collection, which has maybe three hundred pictures in it, my silver treasure box, and my mother's shiny black Mason Pearson brush, which I'd hidden under my pillow so it wouldn't get sold.

Aunt Constance was about to leave the room with these things, but she stopped in the doorway and stood there for a minute; when she turned around, her face was red. There's one more thing, Aunt Constance said. While we are stopping in the city, we will be the guests of Tipsy von Lipp.

I really could hardly believe my ears. Lancasters staying under the same roof as Tipsy Shirley Lipps! Grandmother had warned that she would still find ways to be disappointed with us from beyond the grave. Well, I bet that wherever she was, she was horrified now.

Now, I know what you are thinking, said Aunt Constance. But Mrs. von Lipp very generously offered us a whole wing of her apartment, where we needn't be disturbed—nor intrude on anyone. And we Lancasters must now learn to be financially prudent.

But Belfry says that she's a beast, I told her. And her perfume makes my throat close up.

Aunt Constance tried very hard to look stern like Grandmother.

Not everyone got to grow up the way that we did, she told me. And now that Windy Ridge is gone, you will have to get used to all sorts of people.

It was our last day at Windy Ridge. There was no moon out that night.

CHAPTER THREE
Greenwich Village

Well, I wasn't quite sure how we were going to be able to stuff three big travel trunks, the silver tea set, the big case of silver tableware, the china set, cuckoo clock, wind-up phonograph player, and our other practical things into our old Ford station wagon with the wood panels on the sides. But Belfry came to help and so did our neighbor Mr. Hoots, and between all of us, we shoved and crammed it all in. A big trunk got tied to the top of the car and I was worried that it would slide off while we were driving. It looked like it would squash you flat if it fell on you, but Mr. Hoots said, No, it was tied down really good: we'd be lucky to get it off at all.

When it was time to leave, I told Belfry, I'll send you postcards and maybe some photos too. But he didn't say anything back, and he had a funny look on his face and kept swallowing hard like something was caught in his throat, and he looked kind of skinny when we pulled away and the dust swirled up around him. I wondered if he would ever leave our town, and if he did, would he come back rich and show-offy like Tipsy Lipps? Belfry was poor too. I stared at him in the car mirror and tried hard not to look at the house as it disappeared behind us or at Aunt Constance, who was clearing her throat every two seconds and wiping her eyes with the back of her hand.

We had to go extra-slow on the highway; the car was so heavy that it hovered only a few inches above the ground. Every time we went over a bump, it felt like we'd gone over a boulder, and my legs got pretty dinged up because I had to ride with a jumble of silver candlesticks on the floor in front of me and they kept banging into my knees. To shield her eyes from the sun, Aunt Constance wore a straw hat with a big brim and some orange flowers stuck to it; she also had on her tea-length white gloves. It looked like she was going to a garden party, not on a road trip to find my missing hippie mother. I turned on the radio and wanted to listen to a song called "California Dreamin'," but Aunt Constance turned it off without saying a word, and we spent the rest of the trip to New York City in silence.

By the time we got into the city, Aunt Constance had taken off her gloves and her knuckles were white because she was gripping the wheel so hard. Everyone honked at us, and someone even threw an apple at the car, even though it wasn't her fault that she had to go slow because the trunks were so heavy. Usually Aunt Constance drove only to the grocery store and the flower market to buy begonias for Windy Ridge's porch, and I thought that she was going to cry. We finally found Tipsy Lipps's apartment building, which was very tall and fancy—the sort of place where the doormen have to call you ma'am and bow to you even if they secretly don't like you at all.

When Tipsy Lipps greeted us at her front door, her hair was piled about three feet high on her head and she wore a gold and orange dress that sort of made my eyes hurt.

Why, Constance, she hooted. You look like a country bumpkin in that hat. This is the big city, you know—we have to keep up appearances! I think that I have a lovely caftan you can borrow.

She went on, more to herself than to us: To think that I have Lancasters living under my roof! I never would have dreamed it in a million years! Let me show you to your quarters, darlings.

We followed Tipsy Lipps through about a hundred hallways that all had wallpaper that looked as gold and shiny as her dress. A small army of yapping little white dogs with drag-on-the-ground fur followed us around.

When we finally reached the rooms where we'd be living, Tipsy Lipps went off to powder her nose before cocktail hour and Aunt Constance looked very lost standing there with her straw hat and basket purse. Once the doormen brought our trunks upstairs, Aunt Constance opened one and took out a lace tablecloth and spread it down on a table. Then, on top of that, she put out our Windy Ridge silver tea set.

Now I feel more like myself, she said, and let out a deep breath.

She might have felt better, but I still felt quavery inside, like a breakfast egg that hasn't been cooked enough.

Only this time there was no Windy Ridge front porch to hide under, and no Belfry to hide there with me.

When I woke up the next morning, Aunt Constance had on a long flowery dress and her white gloves and pearls around her neck. I asked if we were going to church, and she said that no, we were going downtown to start looking for my mother. She'd laid out a dress and white knee socks for me to wear, even though it was hot again outside.

It's important to look presentable at all times, Jooooooolia, she told me. People expect it of us, she added.

Really, Constance, said Tipsy Lipps over breakfast as she fed long strips of bacon to her dogs. I can't believe that you're going down to the Village with all of those vile creatures. Do you really think that Rosemary is down there? A Lancaster amidst that riffraff? Artists and hippies. It makes me shudder, darling.

Not all artists are vile creatures, said Aunt Constance. In fact, our family has known some painters with perfectly lovely manners over the years. I'm sure they'll all be very gentlemanly and helpful to us.

They all seem like a bunch of hooligans to me, said Tipsy Lipps, who eyed me and added, Why are you bringing Julia?

I don't think there's any harm in her meeting artists,

Aunt Constance said. And peaceable hippies. The Lan-casters have been patrons of the arts for generations; it's in her blood. And besides, I think that Rosemary should see her child. It might help bring her to—

And then she saw me staring at her and stopped mid-sentence. Everyone was quiet for the rest of the breakfast; the only sound was Tipsy Lipps slurping down her coffee as she made a great show of holding out her pinky from her cup. Her chokey perfume still stuck to us as we rode the elevator downstairs and the doorman hailed us a taxi. When Aunt Constance told the taxi driver to drop us off in the middle of Greenwich Village, please, he turned around, looked at her, then looked at me, and asked if she had the right neighborhood. She told him in a sunny voice that yes, she was sure. He shrugged and the taxi lurched forward.

As the car sped downtown, Aunt Constance opened up her basket purse and pulled out a photograph of my mother wearing her pink pearls and holding a white lily to her chest. I'd seen it before. It was a very old picture, maybe even from before when I was born, and definitely before she let her hair get long and tangled. Aunt Con-stance sighed and tucked the picture back into the purse. I had my camera dangling from my neck as usual.

The driver dropped us off at a place called Washington Square Park. It was filled with people and some of them were carrying signs that said things like:

ONE, TWO, THREE, FOUR

WE DON'T WANT YOUR FAKE WAR

PULL OUR

TROOPS OUT OF

VIETNAM NOW

Put that camera down this instant, Julia, Aunt Constance told me. Don't encourage these people.

What's Vietnam? I asked her.

It's a little country on the other side of the Pacific Ocean, she told me distractedly.

Why is there a war going on there? I wanted to know.

To fight Communists, she replied.

I didn't really know anything about Communists, other than the fact that Grandmother hated them.

What are Communists? I asked. And why are they so bad that we're fighting them in a little country across the Pacific Ocean?

Communists believe that everyone should be equal and that workers should have rights, said Aunt Constance.

Isn't that what Americans believe too? I pressed.

That's quite enough on this topic, Joooooolia, said Aunt Constance, smoothing down the front of her dress. We have other business to attend to.

She peered around the park.

Do not stray from my side, she added, drawing in a deep breath.

On the lawn in front of us sat a bunch of men with long hair. I'd never seen men with long hair before, except for pictures of Jesus. One of them was playing a guitar, and they were passing around a skinny, funny-smelling cigarette, and some of them looked pretty dirty. Aunt Constance slowly walked up to them, and I could practically see her heart beating in her chest.

I'm terribly sorry to bother you, she said, and she fished my mother's picture out of her basket purse and handed it to the men. Have any of you seen this lady? she asked, and added: Her name is Rosemary Lancaster, of the Hudson Valley Lancasters.

The what? asked one of them.

The Hudson Valley Lancasters—is that a butter company or something? snickered another.

Why, no, said Aunt Constance, and faltered. It's just a . . . family.

The long-haired man who was holding the guitar

smiled a wicked smile that reminded me of the Cheshire
Cat in *Alice's Adventures in Wonderland*, and then he
began to strum his guitar. He sang:

> *"A lost little lady*
> *Named Rosemary,*
> *Once docile and sweet,*
> *Now out on the street.*
> *No more pearls, no more gloves,*
> *Only grass and free love."*

Aunt Constance turned bright red and gasped.

We have a child with us, she said. Please mind your
manners.

You're right, said one of the other men with long hair;
he had on sunglasses shaped like little perfectly round
mirrors over his eyes. Where are our manners? Little girl,
would you like some? Sharing is good.

And then he held out the skinny cigarette to me.

No, thank you, I said. Lancasters don't smoke. Grandmother always said that it's unladylike.

They all laughed.

You're both from a different planet, one of them said
to us. You should go back to the mom-and-daughter
knitting club or Junior League, and bake some cakes together or something.

She's not my mother, I informed them, and went on.

My mother is the lady in that picture with the pearls and she's missing. This is my aunt Constance, and she never had any children. Belfry says she's an old maid, but I told him that she's not that old.

Joooooolia, thundered Aunt Constance. That's enough; follow me this instant.

She grabbed my shoulders and marched me away, her hands trembling. We were almost out of the park when one of the long-haired men caught up to us.

Hang on, he told her. I think that I know where that kid's mom might be.

Where is that? asked Aunt Constance warily.

A house on Waverly Place, he said. Look for a pink brick place with black shutters.

Thank you very much, Aunt Constance said, and I could tell that she didn't know whether to believe him or not.

Anyway, there's a lady there who looks just like that little girl, the man said, pointing at me. But she's been on a long trip, so be careful. Who knows what shape she'll be in when you get there?

Well—a trip, said Aunt Constance to me after we'd walked away. She was looking for Waverly Place on a map, and while she looked, she continued in a very distracted way: I wonder where she went—maybe Nantucket. Your mother always liked Nantucket. And a pink house—that sounds quaint.

But when we got to a pink house with black shutters,

it didn't look all that quaint. Paint hung in peels off the front of the little brick building, but there were some pots of brightly colored flowers on the front stoop. A dirty dog lay on the front landing but didn't even raise its head as we walked up the stairs.

This doesn't look too horrible, said Aunt Constance in a crackly voice, and she knocked on the front door.

Yoo-hoo, she called. Rosemary, it's Constance. I'm here with Julia. Are you in there?

The front door opened, but the woman standing on the other side wasn't my mother. She wasn't carrying lilies and she wasn't wearing pearls.

In fact, she wasn't wearing anything but a headband over her long, stringy, unwashed hair.

Aunt Constance quickly covered my eyes with her hand and shoveled me back down the front stairs. Before I knew what was happening, we were in a taxi back up to Tipsy Lipps's apartment. Aunt Constance held her throat with her gloved hand and stared out the window the whole time, her eyes glassy with tears.

That was the last time she took me along down to the Village to look for my mother.

CHAPTER FOUR

The Tipsy Party

Once, when we were studying geography together, my governess taught me about the hottest places on Earth. Like the Sahara Desert or the jungles at the equator. And, of course, the hottest part of all is inside the earth, at the core, where it's all lava and fire and swirling steam.

But I really can't imagine that any of those places is hotter than Tipsy Lipps's apartment in the summertime. First of all, she kept baskets of potpourri everywhere, and every time you opened a window, those smelly petals would blow all over the place, getting stuck in her shaggy fur rugs. So the windows stayed closed at all times and fans were obviously out of the question too.

There was nothing to do but sit around and drip, drip, drip like an old faucet. Every day, Aunt Constance would put on her hat and gloves and disappear into a yellow taxicab, and I knew that she was heading down to Greenwich Village again to look for my mother among naked, headband-wearing ladies and men with Jesus hair. But I would stay put with Tipsy Lipps instead, because Aunt Constance didn't want me to get exposed to any more "morally dissolute persons."

That's how I learned that all of Tipsy Lipps's foot-high hairdos were really wigs, because the moment Aunt Constance left each day, Tipsy Lipps would take her wig off and lie on a gold chaise longue, waving a feather fan over her face. I wished that Belfry could have seen that: she looked just like an old buzzard, if old buzzards wore lipstick and fake eyelashes.

One afternoon, there was a knock at the front door, and then a bunch of movers came in carrying splintery crates with the words *WINDY RIDGE* stamped in red letters on the sides.

Oooo, the Windy Ridge loot! yelled Tipsy Lipps once the workers had opened the crates with crowbars. She went on as she pawed through the boxes: Oh, how marvelous it all is.

Then she scowled: Of course, it all needs to be cleaned. She turned to me and said: Come here, Julia, and help me get all of this silver and china out of the boxes. How could your aunt and grandmother let all of this get so filthy?

I don't know, I told her, and added: They just didn't use it as much anymore once Grandmother went upstairs into her bedroom and stopped coming down.

Well, said Tipsy Lipps, you can bet your boots that it's gonna get used now. Oh yes, oh yes. You know what? I'm going to throw a big dinner party to show off all of my new, shining Lancaster loot. Everyone will positively *drool* with envy! I simply can't believe that this all belongs to *me* now.

She pulled a skinny little fork out of one of the boxes.

What's this used for? she wondered, and turned to me for an answer.

I don't know what came over me then. It was an oyster fork, plain as day, but instead of telling her that, I said:

It's for scratching your head at the dinner table. Grandmother always told us that it's very bad manners to touch your hair with your fingers in the presence of guests.

Tipsy Lipps studied the fork carefully. I suppose that makes sense, she decided.

And what about this? she asked, holding up a silver candle snuffer, which is a little cap dangling from the end of a silver stick; the cap goes over the candle flame and puts it out.

That, I told Tipsy Lipps, is a little hat. You put it on top of your head as everyone's taking their seat at the table, and tip it forward with the stick every time someone sits down or gets up.

Aunt Constance and Grandmother would have been shocked at these whoppers I was making up. Even I was surprising myself, lying to a grown-up like that. Maybe it was seeing Tipsy Lipps pawing through all of our things and calling it loot that made me do it. But it was also kind of fun.

You are going to help me with this dinner party, Tipsy Lipps told me after rummaging through the rest of our Windy Ridge silver. I need to know how all of these fancy things work—every fork and spoon and bowl. None of my guests will ever have seen such a glistening spectacle before. Marie Antoinette herself would be jealous.

I didn't know what this meant or who Marie Antoinette was, but I realized then that I'd backed myself into a corner with my whoppers. Now I'd have to come up with stories about all of that stuff, and I didn't even have Belfry to help me. He was the king of making up whoppers. Tipsy Lipps was staring at me in a way that made me feel like I was a dusty painting she'd found in the attic that was secretly worth a lot of money.

The dinner party was set for exactly a week from that very day.

• • •

I barely got a lick of sleep that week. Tipsy Lipps meant business with this party that was supposed to make Marie Antoinette jealous. Sometimes she would even wake me up in the middle of the night to ask questions like, What did your grandmother use to cover tables at big parties? I told her that no one in their right mind would use the fine Lancaster linen tablecloths that she'd bought as part of the "loot." Instead, I said, Lancasters always used plastic tarps, the kind that painters use on floors and roofs. She looked surprised but didn't question me. Another Tipsy Lipps question: What did the Lancasters serve at the cocktail hour? Oh, Kool-Aid and gin, with lots and lots of sugar mixed in, I told her without even opening my eyes this time.

Usually she whispered these questions to me in a hissy sort of way, so she wouldn't wake up Aunt Constance. Because that was another thing: Aunt Constance was not allowed to know that I was helping Tipsy Lipps get ready for her big party. It was a big secret. Tipsy Lipps wanted everyone to think that she knew how to entertain like a Lancaster on her own, and she wanted Aunt Constance to be as impressed as Marie Antoinette.

Not that Aunt Constance was paying attention to anything that Tipsy Lipps was doing anyway. She didn't seem to be having any luck finding my mother down in the Village, despite spending every day questioning the morally dissolute hippies there. Instead of having dinner with Tipsy Lipps and me, she would go right to her room and lie on her bed with a washcloth over her eyes.

The night of the big dinner party arrived at last. Tipsy Lipps had closed the doors to the dining room so no one could behold it before the right moment, and she was so nervous that I thought her buzzardy head might shoot right off her shoulders.

I will just lie on the floor and *die* if anything goes wrong tonight, she told me.

Apparently all sorts of terribly important people were coming, around twenty of them. As they arrived, my job was to stand at her front door and, every time someone came in, I would give them a goblet of bright red Kool-Aid gin, curtsy, and say:

How do you do, sir? How do you do, madam? I am Julia Lancaster. Welcome to the well-appointed residence of Mrs. Tipsy von Lipp. Please do enjoy your evening.

Aunt Constance was aghast when she saw me greeting the guests this way. She pulled me behind a potted palm tree and demanded to know what on earth I was doing.

I'm helping Tipsy Lipps, I told her. She wants to impress Marie Antoinette with her party.

And before Aunt Constance could say another word, Tipsy Lipps teetered into the middle of the room, holding the candle snuffer on top of her head like it was a little hat. Around her neck dangled a fur stole with about ten little fox heads stuck onto it. (Naturally I'd told her that important hostesses always wore fox-fur stoles with the heads still on them, and Tipsy had bought a bunch of them from a taxidermist downtown and even sewed them on herself.)

She raised the snuffer into the air and stood there with her arm up like the Statue of Liberty for a minute before declaring:

Darlings, I welcome you to my table.

And with that, she ran over to the dining room doors and threw them open.

All of the guests gasped. The room had been made over to look like the inside of a circus tent—which is exactly how Grandmother used to decorate for all of our summer soirées, I'd told her. Bales of scratchy hay had been stacked up against the wall. An old monkey wearing a little red hat and jacket stood miserably in the doorway, holding a bowl of olives. It screeched when Tipsy Lipps tried to pat it on the head.

Has she gone *mad*? whispered one woman to her husband.

This is without a doubt the tackiest thing I've ever seen, whispered another.

Darlings, Tipsy Lipps sang out. Tonight is a very special occasion. I'm not sure if you *know* this, but I have been such good friends with the illustrious Lancasters for ever so long. Why, we go back simply *ages*. As you may have heard, the family has fallen on hard times.

Aunt Constance's face flushed a deep red.

Well, I was absolutely in *despair* when I heard that they were being forced to sell their ancestral home, Windy Ridge, Tipsy Lipps went on. So I swept upstate and bought it, to help my dear, treasured friends.

It was the Christian thing to do, she added solemnly, and conjured up a modest blush.

Tonight's party is in honor of poor, dear Constance Lancaster and poor, dear little Julia Lancaster, she proclaimed. Windy Ridge lives on, dears—here in my apartment. So take heart—and she gave me a couple of hard pats on the shoulder. Then she tipped the candle snuffer off her head and bid us all to take our seats.

The moment everyone sat down, the monkey threw the bowl of olives into the air and everyone got sprayed with olive juice.

Bad monkey! Bad monkey! cried Tipsy Lipps.

Why do you have that putrid animal here in the first

place? one of the guests demanded, wiping olive juice from her eyes.

Why, all of the finest society hostesses have monkey servers at their supper parties, said Tipsy Lipps, but she gave me a terrible look when she said it and I could tell that she was beginning to suspect that I'd been pulling her leg all along.

Just then two servers wearing clown costumes lugged an enormous pie into the room and heaved it onto the dining room table.

Oh, wonderful—the main course, croaked Tipsy Lipps.

I sat straight up on my chair; my heart pounded. I had told her that Lancasters always serve songbird pies at their parties, but I didn't think that old Tipsy would actually go ahead and have one made. Boy, was I wrong. She took one of our long silver Lancaster knives and slit the crust down the middle, and suddenly a flock of birds shot out of the pie and flew like a swarm of bees around the room. All of the ladies screamed their heads off. Then the birds really went crazy and one of them even got caught in Tipsy's wig, lifting it right off her head and dropping it back down again sideways.

Well, it's awfully late, yelled one man even though it was only seven o'clock. I have to be going. Thank you for a lovely evening, he added, and practically ran out of the room.

All of the other guests stood up and followed him. Poor Tipsy Lipps tipped the candle snuffer from her head over and over again as each person escaped her dinner party, and when the last one left, she flung open the window and shooed all of the songbirds out into the city sky.

You are a ghastly child, Julia Lancaster, cried Tipsy Lipps, and then she ran out of the room too.

Aunt Constance and I were the only ones left sitting at the table. She stared at me and I knew that she knew what I'd done, and I squeezed my eyes shut and cringed, waiting for her to really let me have it.

But when I opened my eyes a crack, I saw that she was trying not to smile.

Well, Jooooooolia, she said finally. At least you know what it takes to make a memorable dinner party. Not everyone has that gift.

And we went off to bed.

Two things happened after the Tipsy party:

1. Tipsy Lipps didn't come out of her bedroom for three days. And when she finally did come out, she told her servants to pack up the Windy Ridge loot and send it to Sotheby's auction house, where it would get sold to somebody new. Then she told Aunt Constance that she'd

decided to redecorate her entire apartment and that there wouldn't be room for us anymore, so we would have to find someplace else to stay. She wouldn't even look at me.

2. That same day, Aunt Constance came back from Greenwich Village very excited and told me that she finally had a lead. A non–morally dissolute hippie had recognized the picture of my mother at last and told Aunt Constance where we might be able to find her. The good news: it was not in Greenwich Village. The bad news: she had apparently gone all the way down south with a bunch of other hippies to a city named New Orleans to learn about something called voodoo, so we would have to get back into the car with our trunks and practical-travel things and go down there to find her.

As we drove out of New York City the next morning, I asked Aunt Constance what voodoo was. She gripped the steering wheel extra-hard and said we'd find out soon enough.

PART TWO
Down South

CHAPTER FIVE

Paw Paw

Somewhere along the way, I think in New Jersey, we stopped at a gas station and bought a map of the United States of America. It practically covered the whole hood of our car when you opened it up, so Aunt Constance would only let me open it a little bit at a time while we were driving. When I got tired of looking out the window, I looked at the map instead and made a list of the funniest town names. Some of my favorites:

- *Hot Coffee, Mississippi*
- *Truth or Consequences, New Mexico*
- *Mischief, Texas*
- *Gunslinger, Missouri*
- *High and Mighty, Oklahoma*
- *Loveless, Arkansas*

When we got to Maryland, Aunt Constance let us stop at a Howard Johnson's to have strawberry ice cream and I wrote down some of the best town names on a postcard with a picture of some crabs on the front and mailed it off to Belfry:

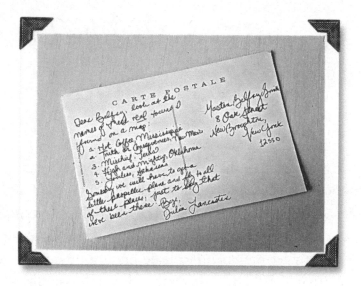

Soon we stopped going through cities and started going through fields and forests.

We're in a state called West Virginia, Aunt Constance told me.

It's pretty, I said, looking out at all of the pine trees.

No, it's a beastly place, said Aunt Constance, who added that she was very keen to get through it as quickly as possible, and that's when she drove right over a big hole in the road and black smoke started to come out from under the hood. After a while, a tow truck came and dragged our car into the nearest town, which was called Paw Paw. By then it was too late to put this name on my postcard to Belfry—I'd sent it already—but I swore to remember it and add it to the next one.

This is what was in Paw Paw:

- *A general store that sold flour, candy, soda, animal traps, and guns;*
- *A gas station with one pump;*
- *A restaurant called Mary Lou's Kitchen that looked like it had been closed since around 1932;*
- *A "laundry-mat" with coin-operated machines and a blind owner, who sat on the front porch with a cane and a little radio with a hand crank.*

And that's about it.

The man at the gas station told Aunt Constance it would take him a couple of days to fix our car. Aunt Constance looked very worried and asked where on earth we would stay for two whole days when there wasn't a single hotel in Paw Paw. I piped up and said that maybe there was a teepee that we could buy in the general store, and that I'd always wanted to try living in a teepee. But she got very cross and told me to shush:

she wasn't going to live in a teepee. Then the gas station man said that there was one family that took in boarders, whatever that meant, and he wrote down an address for Aunt Constance. When we got to the house with that address, Aunt Constance looked up at it and said under her breath that she would never forgive my mother as long as she lived.

Some of the front steps were missing and a one-eyed cat lazed in the sunshine on the splintery porch. There wasn't a doorbell, so Aunt Constance knocked gently on the door and wrung the paper with the address on it into a stringy mess while we waited for an answer.

Soon a woman carrying a baby and wearing an apron opened the door and informed Aunt Constance:

Don't try to sell us something—not even a Bible. We're dead broke here.

We're not selling anything, said Aunt Constance. My niece and I are looking for a place to stay for a couple of days. We heard that you take in boarders.

Oh, said the woman, looking us up and down. We do have a room out back. Come and have a look at it.

The room out back was in a sort of shack that had sad red curtains drooping across the windows and two little cots inside. There was another cat in there too. It had both of its eyes, but its fur was coming out in clumps.

Aunt Constance looked like she was about to cry,

but there wasn't anyplace else to stay in Paw Paw besides a teepee or else our broken car, so she put on her politest face and told the woman that we would take it. Then the gas station man brought over our luggage, including the three travel trunks and all of our silver. After that there was barely any room to move in our shack; the cat curled up in one of our suitcases and went to sleep.

Grandmother is definitely disapproving from heaven right now, I told Aunt Constance.

She started to laugh until a few tears slid down her cheeks.

• • •

When we woke up on the cots the next morning, Aunt Constance looked at me while I got dressed.

You need a bath, Joooooolia, she told me.

She went inside the main house to ask if we could use the bathtub. When she came out again a minute later, she was carrying two threadbare towels and a gray cake of soap.

There's no plumbing in the house, she said miserably, so we have to bathe in the creek back in the woods.

I grabbed my camera and brought it along because you never know what you might see in a creek in a place called Paw Paw.

Moss covered the bank of the creek, which felt nice under my bare feet. I started to take off all of my clothes, but Aunt Constance made me keep on a silk slip and she did too.

You never know who's out there watching, she said, and no matter where we are, we are ladies and we are Lancasters.

The creek water was icy cold, even though it was late summer and the air was noon-hot already. With her pale pink-white skin and red hair, I thought that Aunt Constance looked a lot like a wood nymph. We passed the cake of soap back and forth as we washed ourselves in that cold rush of Paw Paw water; minnows and water bugs skittered around our ankles.

For breakfast, Dorothea—the house's owner—gave us a plate of corn bread with nothing on it. There was nothing to do after that but wait to hear from the gas station man about our car. Aunt Constance found a copy of *Pride and Prejudice* in one of the travel trunks and sat on the back porch pretending to read it. I pulled out our map and rustled it around so much that she got annoyed and told me to go play in the woods for a spell.

I wandered back to the creek and waded out into the middle. All sorts of fish were swimming there—silvery and slick, and fatter than any of the people we'd seen in Paw Paw. I tried to catch a few using the edge of my dress as a net, but they kept getting away.

Then a voice behind me said:

I can catch them with my bare hands.

I spun around, and there on the bank stood a girl about eight years old. At least I thought she was a girl from her voice, but her hair was cut in jagged, short tufts all over her head, as if the haircut had been done with a knife and not a pair of scissors. Plus, she wore overalls and nothing else.

Who are you? I asked.

I'm Jack, said the kid. I live in the house where you're boarding.

Are you a girl? I asked her, even though I knew that it sounded sort of rude, but I wanted to be absolutely sure one way or the other. She said yes, she was indeed a girl, and she didn't seem embarrassed at all.

But why is your name Jack if you're a girl? I asked her.

It's short for *Jacqueline,* said Jack. I just like *Jack* better, so I made everyone call me that, ever since I was little.

I said that made perfect sense, and after that it was understood that we were friends.

Jack waded out into the creek and came up next to me. Where'd you get that? she asked, and pointed at my camera.

It's mine, I told her. It was a present.

Nice present, she told me. I only saw one before, when a man came through town from a newspaper and took pictures of us and said it was a story about poor people. My mother cried for about a week after that.

I won't take your picture, I promised her, and told her that I just wanted a picture of the fish.

Stand extra-still, she told me.

We were very quiet for a minute, and then a big silver fish came sliding through the water toward us, and quick as lightning, Jack darted forward and grabbed the fish in her hands. It wiggled and writhed and gleamed in a beam of sunshine that came through the trees, but she didn't let go. Instead she brought it over to the mossy bank and whacked it on a rock, and when it was still, she laid it out on some fern fronds. And then she caught three more the same way, each one bigger than the last.

Now we have dinner for my family and for you and your aunt too, Jack said. We were sitting on the bank by then, letting our clothes dry.

I've never eaten fish right from a stream, I told her. At Windy Ridge, we always got our food at the store, or Grandmother would order it from catalogs and it would come in boxes from all over the country and the world.

We barely get anything from the store, said Jack, only stuff like flour and salt. We mostly eat what I can catch out here in the woods.

Like what else besides fish? I asked her.

Oh, anything, she said. Like possums—and once I shot a deer with an arrow.

I tried to imagine Tipsy Lipps eating a possum caught in the woods—or Aunt Constance, for that matter—and my mind wouldn't even let me do it. Just then I saw a frog hopping along the edge of the bank.

If you caught that frog, we could make *cuisses de grenouille,* I told Jack.

She just stared at me. Make what? she asked.

Frog legs, I said. They eat them in Paris all the time. And Grandmother used to have a big French cookbook with a gold cover that told you how to make them here in America too.

Jack looked very puzzled and said, They eat them where?

So I told her they eat them in a fancy country across the Atlantic Ocean, and then added that they eat snails there too. Jack looked like she might throw up, but I told her that even kings and queens eat them, and that they were actually very tasty when seasoned well and prepared intelligently, which is what Grandmother always used to say. Jack told me that her family was always hungry and would usually eat anything, but she didn't know if they would try snails.

But I think I might try a snail, she said after a minute. After all, how bad can they be if kings and queens eat them?

Then I had an idea.

Let's make a big Paris feast for your mother and my

aunt tonight, I told Jack, and catch everything we need in the woods and the stream. At the very least, your mother will like the fish and Aunt Constance will like the snails and everyone will be happy.

Jack agreed that it was a swell idea, and we got to work.

It took all day to get ready for the feast. Jack caught five more silvery fish, and she made a campfire near the creek bank to cook them. I pulled snails off the rocks in the stream, and then we both waded through the water, trying to catch frogs. We caught only three measly ones, but I said that six frog legs were probably enough. Jack put them in a tall wooden bucket, and they croaked and leaped around but not enough to turn the bucket over.

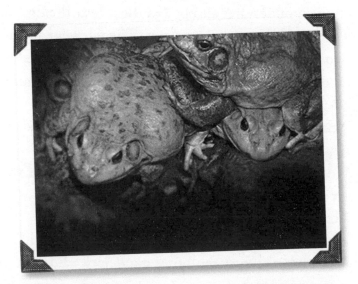

Then Jack said she knew where we could find mushrooms too, and we walked through the woods to a dell where mushrooms grew on tree trunks like ruffles on a dress collar. Jack showed me the difference between mushrooms you could eat and the ones that would kill you or make you see funny things, and we picked a bunch of them and carried them back to the campfire in the hem of my dress.

Soon the shadows grew long in the woods and the light started to thin and fade. Jack began cooking the fish, and she had to kill the frogs because I didn't know how to, and then she cut off their legs and put them on a stick to roast over the fire. I didn't think that this was how Grandmother's French cookbook at Windy Ridge said to make them, but I didn't say anything. We put the snails in a pot of water and boiled them over the fire, and Jack roasted the mushrooms too. Then I went up into our boarders' shack with the red curtains and pulled out some of our practical-travel things to make a beautiful forest-floor picnic.

Jack looked at our silver glistening there on the dirt.

Are you rich? she asked me.

We were once, I said. But not anymore. I think we're pretty poor now. We had to sell our house.

That's too bad, said Jack. We're poor too.

I asked her if she and Dorothea minded not having any running water in the house, and Jack said that no, they were used to it.

We could live with my grandparents if we wanted to, said Jack. They have a house with water, and lights too. But my mother likes living out here in the woods. She doesn't like being told what to do by anyone, and we have everything that we need. It's home.

My mother says that everything in life is a choice, she added.

Well, I thought about that for a minute, and I decided that I didn't know if I thought Jack's mother was right about that. It wasn't Aunt Constance's choice to sell off Windy Ridge and all of its contents to Tipsy Lipps, for example. And it didn't seem that I'd been given any choice about coming along on this trip. Not that I was complaining; I liked being in the car and seeing all of these new places. I might even be getting smarter than Belfry with all of this travel. But no one had ever asked me if I wanted to go.

By then the feast was ready, so Jack and I went up to the house and got Aunt Constance and Dorothea and the baby, and we led them down into the woods. I had put out all of our silver candlesticks along the path and luckily it wasn't windy in the woods, so the candles flickered prettily in all of that blue evening light. Aunt Constance and Jack's mother gasped when they saw what we'd done.

This is what God's table must look like in heaven, said Jack's mother.

Fat fireflies came and hovered around us, and we all sat

down on the Windy Ridge Oriental carpets I'd laid out on the moss and ate the forest feast. Jack's mother rocked the baby in her arms when we were done eating and sang her a lullaby:

"Summertime
And the livin' is easy.
Fish are jumpin'
And the cotton is high."

The moon rose and we could see it through the tree-tops, and it shone in silver streaks on the stream. It was too beautiful to go back inside, so Jack's mother sang more lullabies to the baby, and it must have hypnotized everyone, because all five of us slept out there on the banks of Paw Paw Creek that night, the fire crackling quietly until it smoldered out and the stream keeping up the lullaby after we all fell asleep.

Not only did the Paw Paw gas station man fix our car, he somehow made it go higher up off the ground so Aunt Constance could run over holes in the road without making black smoke come out from under the hood. He loaded up our trunks onto the car, and we said goodbye to Jack and Dorothea and the baby. I turned around and watched them as we drove away, and suddenly I realized that I was jealous of Jack, even though she barely had anything in this world, not even a toilet or a lightbulb hanging from the ceiling in the kitchen. Nothing. But I was jealous anyway, because Jack had a mother and a home, and I did not. And then I started to think about how Dorothea thought that everything is a choice in life.

Aunt Constance, I said.

Yes, Julia, she replied.

Why did you decide not to have your own little girl? I asked her.

Aunt Constance didn't say anything for a long time. I expected her to tell me that Lancasters never asked such personal questions, it was rude to do so, but instead she said this:

It wasn't really my choice. I stayed at Windy Ridge to help take care of the house, and then suddenly Grandmother was old, and I had to take care of her too.

So, I was right, I said to myself. Not everything is a choice. Out loud, I said:

But who will take care of you?

I will have to take care of myself, said Aunt Constance.

It was quiet then for a little while, until I asked her:

And will you be taking care of me too?

Then there were only the noises of the car engine and the whoosh of air outside the window and my own heart beating as I waited for the answer to my question.

For now I am taking care of you, Julia, she told me finally.

Why only for now? I asked, because now that

Grandmother was gone and my mother was gone too, the list of other people to take care of me seemed pretty short.

Because I've never been a mother, and I'm not sure that I'd be good at it, Aunt Constance said, and seemed very uncomfortable, like she did when she had to talk about money.

Let's just enjoy the scenery now, she added, and because she looked like she might cry, I didn't ask her any more questions, even though the cloud-over-sun feeling had come back. So I stared out the window at the blur of pine trees whizzing by, trying to count them, until I fell asleep.

CHAPTER SIX

White Lies

It took us many days to get from Paw Paw to New Orleans. We had to drive down, down, down through Kentucky (lots of horse farms) and then through Tennessee (very green). When we got into Mississippi, we drove along the bluffs of the Mississippi River and we had to stay at more boarding houses along the way, because none of the tiny river towns in Mississippi had hotels in them. I showed Aunt Constance the map and told her that there were lots of big cities in Mississippi that probably had hotels, like Jackson and Hattiesburg and Oxford, but Aunt Constance wouldn't go near a Mississippi city.

Those towns are simply too dangerous because of the violence over giving Negroes the vote, she told me. And I don't fancy getting caught in the middle of a big riot.

Especially with all of our Windy Ridge finery, she added.

I asked her why white people in Mississippi were against giving Negroes the vote.

Well, there's a lot of ignorance down here, she replied. And ignorance mixed with too many guns is like a badly mixed, too-strong gin and tonic: it's best to just leave it alone.

She got so worked up that I was worried she would drive over another hole in the road, so I stopped talking to her about the vote. I think she was very relieved when we finally got into Louisiana and then to New Orleans, and we pulled up in front of a big mansion in the Garden District where we'd be staying:

For the first time since we left Windy Ridge, Aunt Constance could take a little break and not think about hippies or city violence or broken-down cars, and instead she could think about the things she used to think about at Windy Ridge, like teatime and white gloves and when to say *who* instead of *whom*.

She slept for about three days straight.

For the duration of our New Orleans visit, we were the guests of a lady named Prunella Foxworth, who had gone to Miss Horton's School with Grandmother about a hundred years ago.

Now, Julia, there's something you should know, said Aunt Constance when we had first pulled up in front of the house. Mrs. Foxworth is an old-guard New Orleans grande dame—so while we're here, you must behave accordingly.

What's a grande dame? I asked her.

A rather flamboyant older woman of means who has lots of opinions, replied Aunt Constance as she straightened her hat in front of a mirror.

This didn't make things much clearer to me, but when I saw Prunella Foxworth for myself, I decided that *old-guard New Orleans grande dame* meant an old lady who was quite fat and wore lots of face powder and big hats and flowered dresses and kept a little servant-summoning brass bell attached to her wrist with a silk ribbon.

Aunt Constance told me not to mention anything about voodoo to Mrs. Foxworth; it might upset her, she said. After all, Mrs. Foxworth was a proper old lady who played bridge. And then she instructed me that Mrs. Foxworth was also not to be told that my mother had run off to become a hippie who then came to New Orleans to learn about voodoo.

If she asks, we are simply here to tour the city, Aunt Constance said.

But I thought that Lancasters never lied, I said.

We're not lying, she told me. We're just not telling the whole truth. Or anyway, it's just a white lie. White lies never hurt anyone. In fact, white lies are meant to preserve other people's feelings.

I promised not to say anything and also kept it to myself that I'd learned a little bit about voodoo on my own: while we were staying as boarders in one small Mississippi town, I'd walked over to the public library one afternoon while Aunt Constance was taking a nap. I marched right up to the dictionary section and pulled down a book.

Here was the official definition of voodoo:

> **voo·doo [voo-doo], noun**
> 1. A polytheistic religion practiced chiefly by West Indians, deriving from African cult worship and containing elements borrowed from the Catholic religion.
> 2. A person who practices this religion.
> 3. Black magic; sorcery.

The library had other books on voodoo too, and no one noticed when I sat down in the corner with a big pile of them, even though voodoo seemed kind of scary and not really what Grandmother would call Appropriate Reading for Youths. I think you can get away with more in New Orleans than you can in New York. Anyway, I learned a lot. In voodoo, there apparently aren't any church priests who make you eat dry crackers and sit still on long, hard wooden benches and talk about the Holy Ghost. Instead there are these wild voodoo queens, who can put hexes on people and tell the future. And you get taught all sorts of things, like how to ward off witches by putting a broomstick across a doorway at night or how to give someone a headache just by turning a picture of them upside down.

All of this information seemed very useful, so I wrote it down on a postcard and tucked it into my luggage, just in case. I also checked the books to see if there were any voodoo spells that helped you find missing people, or maybe a spell that made other people want to take care of you. But there was nothing there like that. We'd just have to find my mother the old-fashioned way.

By asking around.

We were given a big breakfast feast on our first full day at Mrs. Foxworth's house. Her servants, Moody and Bun, brought in a basket of steaming biscuits smothered in honey butter, oyster-and-cream omelets, a big stack of hickory bacon, and tar-black coffee swirled with thick steamed milk.

How do you intend to spend the day, dear? Mrs. Foxworth asked as she gulped down approximately a bucket of the coffee.

Aunt Constance told her that we were going to go to a rose-judging contest at the botanical gardens. But I knew that Aunt Constance was telling a white lie to Mrs. Foxworth and that she really intended to go look for voodoo queens and see if any of them had been teaching voodoo to my mother.

Well, said Mrs. Foxworth, patting her lips with a lace napkin, I think that sounds like a splendid idea. I think that I'll come along with you, Constance. There's nothing more invigorating than spending the day in the company of regal roses.

Aunt Constance looked stricken, but then there was nothing to do but put on her big straw hat and wait for Mrs. Foxworth to put on a pound of white face powder and at least five pounds of pearls too. So off we all went to a boring rose fair, which was filled with lots of old-guard New Orleans grandes dames who looked just like Mrs. Foxworth, and we had to hang around there until dinnertime.

The next morning, Aunt Constance tried again. She said to Mrs. Foxworth:

You've gone through so much trouble to entertain us, dear Prunella. I think that I'll take Julia today to the library so we can spend the day reading quietly and leave you in peace.

Mrs. Foxworth put down a forkful of omelet Creole and stared at Aunt Constance.

You know, Constance—that is a wonderful idea, she exclaimed. I have not set foot in our local library for more than ten years. There's nothing more refreshing than spending the day amidst great works of literature. I think that I shall accompany you.

So, on went the powder; on went the pearls; on went the hat; and all three of us went out the door. Aunt Constance's mouth made a shape like an upside-down U. She spent most of the day finding books for Mrs. Foxworth about Confederate soldiers, and I snuck away to another part of the library and read more about voodoo queens and learned how to put a curse on someone by putting a drop of chicken blood into their soup.

At breakfast the next day, Aunt Constance leaned forward and clapped her hand onto my forehead.

Why, Julia Lancaster, she said. You're burning up.

No, I'm not, I said, and suddenly I felt a poke under the table.

Prunella, I think I'll take her to the doctor, said Aunt Constance.

Mrs. Foxworth put down her beignet and wiped away the powdered sugar from her mouth.

Oh dear, how terrible to feel unwell so far from home, she said. I shall most certainly accompany you to the doctor, you poor things.

Oh, please don't concern yourself with us, pleaded Aunt Constance. And besides, you might get sick yourself: you know how doctors' offices are.

Hogwash, scoffed Mrs. Foxworth, and then all three of us trundled off to her doctor, who told Aunt Constance and Mrs. Foxworth that there wasn't a blessed thing wrong with me and that I was probably crying wolf to get attention.

Well, as I live and breathe, bristled Mrs. Foxworth as her chauffeur whisked us back home in her long black car. In my day, little girls who told lies went to bed without dinner. That's how we should deal with you as well. Shame on you for worrying your aunt like that.

So that night I was sent to bed without dinner. I turned off all the lights in my room and looked out over the city, which was bathed in moonlight.

And I wondered if my mother could really be someplace nearby. Maybe she was doing the exact same thing.

CHAPTER SEVEN

Voodoo Queens

It turned out that Mrs. Foxworth's servants, Moody and Bun, were sisters. I learned this from eavesdropping on them later that night. My room in Mrs. Foxworth's house was right above the kitchen, and I woke up at three in the morning and heard voices through the floor, and then I started to smell delicious cooking smells, and my stomach started to rumble from not eating any dinner. So I tiptoed down the maids' staircase and sat behind the swinging back door to the kitchen and waited for Moody and Bun to leave the room so I could run in and snatch up a biscuit and maybe even some of whatever they were cooking.

But they never left the room. Instead they kept cooking and talking and talking and cooking some more, and then I heard the *slap, slap, slap* of cards being laid down on a table and bits of conversation that went like this:

Bun: What a bad sign. You pulled out the
tower. That means a disaster is comin'.

Moody: But it's upside down. That's a good sign.

Bun: Oh, that's okay, then. The tower upside
down means that even if disaster's
comin', you can handle it.

The cooking smells started to get so good that I almost
started drooling like Belfry's stinky old mutt, Boris, who
always left a trail of spittle wherever he went. Finally it
was all too much, and I decided to try to sneak in without
Moody and Bun hearing me by opening the swinging
door a centimeter at a time and grabbing the closest food
from the counter.

So I started opening the door so slowly that it seemed like
it was barely moving, and I congratulated myself on having
such a steady hand, and soon it was open just enough for
me to squeeze through. But then the moment I started to
squeeze through it, there on the other side stood Moody and
Bun in their bathrobes and their hair all wound up in tur-
bans, and Bun had a rolling pin in one hand, and neither of
them looked at all happy to see me. Moody reached out and
grabbed me by the ear and marched me over to the table.

You sit down, child, she thundered. What were you
thinkin', sneakin' in here like that? We were liable to
think you were a burglar and beat you black-and-blue.

I'm hungry, I told them.

And I added that I hadn't meant to spy on them, which

was sort of a lie, because I liked hearing their strange conversation. Moody and Bun stared down at me, and I was afraid that they would go get Mrs. Foxworth, who probably looked pretty scary when she wasn't wearing all of her daytime powder and lipstick. But instead Bun sashayed over to the stove and scooped something out of a pot into a bowl and set it down in front of me.

That's shrimp étouffée, she told me, and it was the best thing I'd ever tasted. I ate two bowls of it.

What are those? I asked them, pointing to the cards on the table. They didn't look like regular cards that we used at Windy Ridge to play gin and bridge and hearts. Instead Bun and Moody's cards had pictures all over them and for some reason they kind of scared me.

Those are tarot cards, Moody said. They tell the future.

When I took a picture of them, both Moody and Bun let out such a gasp that I almost dropped my camera.

That's probably real bad luck, taking a picture of the tarot, Moody said.

Oh, I said. I didn't know, I added, and asked, Is there any way to undo the bad luck now?

I don't know, said Moody. Maybe just tear up the picture when you get it back, just to be sure.

I said that I would, but I looked at the cards again and thought they were too pretty for me to tear up the picture. Anyway, we Lancasters had already had such bad luck that a little more likely wouldn't do any harm.

And then Moody asked me if I had any questions about the future that I wanted to ask.

Well, this seemed very serious. I didn't want to ask the cards just anything, after all. So I thought about it for a few minutes and wrote my questions down on a piece of paper:

> *Am I going to marry Belfry someday?*
> *Is Aunt Constance going to send me to Miss Horton's*
> *   School when we are done with our trip?*
> *Are we going to find my mother?*

Moody shuffled the cards and told me to touch them, so I did. She laid down five cards.

You ain't gonna marry Belfry, she said.

I slumped down in my chair. I always thought that

I'd marry Belfry someday. I was so used to him and liked him so much, and really couldn't imagine liking someone else nearly as much.

Then Moody laid down five more cards.

Yes, you're goin' to Miss Horton's School.

I slumped down even farther. So, I guess that was the answer to my question about who was going to take care of me. Miss Horton would get that job.

Five more cards got slapped down on the table. Moody looked at them and was quiet.

Well, what do they say? I asked. Are we going to find my mother?

Well, this doesn't happen a lot, but the cards are saying both yes and no, said Moody.

Bun looked over at the cards also and both ladies studied them for a while. Then Moody gathered them up suddenly and put them away.

No one's got all the answers all the time, she said, and then she gave me a biscuit and sent me back up to bed.

A miracle happened the next morning: Mrs. Foxworth woke up with a stomachache that she'd gotten from eating a bad crabmeat *maison* the night before at Galatoire's Restaurant. Aunt Constance tried not to look overjoyed as she tucked a frilly sheet up under Mrs. Foxworth's double chin, but the moment Mrs. Foxworth drifted off to sleep, Aunt Constance put on her straw hat and I knew she was going out to look for my mother at the places where voodoo was taught. I followed her out onto the porch, my camera around my neck as usual.

Please take me too, I begged.

Absolutely not, she told me.

But I read that voodoo is just a religion, I said. And it's good to learn about different religions, isn't it? And to learn about new places too? I want to see New Orleans.

Aunt Constance didn't say anything then, and I knew that my foot was probably through the door.

I'll come back here right away if anything bad happens, I promised, and after a few more minutes of this, Aunt Constance reluctantly agreed to let me come, and part of me wondered if she just said yes because secretly she was a little scared to go by herself.

We got out of a taxi in a part of New Orleans called the French Quarter, which had lots of pretty, small buildings colored like pastel tea cakes and flowers pouring off their balconies.

Suddenly a police car pulled up next to us. The policeman driving the car was very fat and had a mustache like a broom. He rolled down his window and leaned out.

Good morning, ladies, he said.

Good morning, sir, said Aunt Constance.

Has either of you seen a recess monkey walking around these parts? asked the policeman.

Aunt Constance paused, and she replied, I beg your pardon?

A recess monkey, repeated the policeman, and he showed us a picture of a skinny monkey and then added: He's got a collar with bells around his neck.

No, said Aunt Constance. No, we haven't seen a recess monkey with a bell collar.

Well, be careful if you do, because he bites, said the policeman, rolling up his window. And with that, he drove away.

Aunt Constance's hand went to her throat.

Well, I never, she said.

We walked up and down the streets of the Quarter until Aunt Constance saw a sign that interested her:

Aunt Constance closed her eyes and took a deep breath before we walked in through the door.

The room was filled with red light and cigarette smoke, and I thought that this was how hell might look. Behind a round table in the middle of the room sat a woman with scrawny hands, a high pillar of fabric wound around her head.

Excuse me, ma'am, but are you Saint Marie Celeste? asked Aunt Constance politely.

Suddenly the woman tilted her head back and rolled her eyes toward the ceiling. Then she pointed at Aunt Constance.

You, said the woman in a crackly voice. I have been waiting for you to arrive.

I'm not sure what you mean, said Aunt Constance.

You are from a very old New Orleans family, said the woman. And your name begins with a *T*.

Well, no, actually, said Aunt Constance. You are clearly confusing me with someone else.

Hush, said the voodoo woman. You came to me in a dream. You are searching for something.

I whispered to Aunt Constance that this woman was the phoniest phony I'd ever seen, but Aunt Constance sort of swatted in my direction and then fished the pearls-and-lily picture of my mother out of her basket purse.

Have you seen this lady? Aunt Constance asked the woman.

She squinted at the photograph.

Ohhh yes, she said. Many times.

What's her name, then? I demanded.

Her name is . . . Sally, the woman said.

No, it isn't, I told her.

That's what she said her name was when she came to see me, said the woman quickly, but I didn't believe her. Then she added: I can tell you where she is—for a price.

Aunt Constance asked how much, and the woman said ten dollars, and the money changed hands. Then the woman made a big show of rolling her eyes back into her head and chanting a bunch of nonsense and then she sat up straight as a poker.

She has joined the circus and left town, said the woman.

That's the dumbest thing I've ever heard, I hollered. Give us back our ten dollars.

But Saint Marie Celeste wouldn't give the money back, of course, and we left in a hurry, and the pink climbed up into Aunt Constance's cheeks. We marched around the Quarter and went to four other places like Saint Marie Celeste's Voodoo Parlor, and every one of them told us something different about where my mother was. Aunt Constance spent all of the money she had in her basket purse, so we had to walk back to Mrs. Foxworth's house instead of hailing a taxi, and we were no smarter and a lot poorer than when we'd left.

• • •

That night, I heard Bun and Moody in the kitchen again. I went downstairs to see if they'd give me a taste of whatever they were cooking. This time it was a crawfish gumbo and while I was eating it, they asked me where Aunt Constance and I had been the whole day.

I'm not allowed to say, I told them. Or at least, I'm not allowed to tell Mrs. Foxworth.

Oh, we never tell her anything, said Moody.

We'll be silent as the grave, added Bun.

So I told them that my mother was a hippie who'd supposedly come down to New Orleans to study voodoo, and that we'd gone to a bunch of voodoo houses in the Quarter to try to find her, and that they'd all been a bunch of fakes, and that we were at a dead end.

Suddenly the kitchen door swung open and there stood Mrs. Foxworth, clad in a frilly robe, her face slathered in white cold cream.

That's because you've been looking in all the wrong places, she declared, and then she swished into the kitchen.

Moody and Bun shot to their feet.

Can we get you anything, Mrs. Foxworth? asked Bun.

Yes, please serve me a bowl of that crawfish gumbo, said Mrs. Foxworth, plumping herself down at the table next to me.

Why didn't you tell me the real reason you were here? Mrs. Foxworth asked me. Apparently I wasn't the only expert behind-the-door eavesdropper in the house. I said that

Aunt Constance thought she was an old-guard New Orleans grande dame and therefore might get upset if she knew that we were consorting with voodoo types in the Quarter.

Child, you Lancasters have been piddling around with amateurs, Mrs. Foxworth informed me in between big bites of gumbo. If only you'd confided in me, she added. Then she finished her gumbo and announced:

Tomorrow I will personally take you to Madame Flavie Batilde.

Moody and Bun both gasped at the same time.

You mean she's still alive? asked Bun.

Very much so, said Mrs. Foxworth. Then she told me that Madame Flavie Batilde was the most famous voodoo queen who'd ever lived in New Orleans and maybe even anywhere in the world. Then Moody added that Madame Batilde allowed so few people to see her that lots of folks didn't even think she was a real person, just a made-up legend.

Well, she lets *me* see her, Mrs. Foxworth said. She went on:

Every Thursday afternoon at four o'clock, we drink a glass of absinthe together, and she tells me everything that's going to happen around the world. In fact, she predicted the shootings of both of those poor Kennedy boys and Dr. Martin Luther King.

Moody and Bun looked terribly impressed. Mrs. Foxworth let this information sink in, and after a minute she turned to me and said gravely:

If anyone on earth knows where to find your mother, it's Madame Batilde.

First of all, Madame Flavie Batilde's house was nothing like the fake voodoo parlors in the Quarter. It sort of reminded me of the kind of place a grandmother might live, one who likes doilies and knitting and quiet evenings. When we got there, Madame was sitting on the pale gray front porch behind a curtain of night-blooming jasmine. Standing in front of her on a silver tray was a bottle with something green in it and three glasses—one for her, and one each for Mrs. Foxworth and Aunt Constance. For me she had a big crystal glass of iced tea that was so sweet, it made my teeth throb.

Second of all: Madame looked nothing like the phony voodoo queens who'd rooked Aunt Constance out of all that money. Instead, she wore a housedress with little flowers on it and had bare feet and smelled like lilies of the valley. She had a big gold front tooth and once in a while it glinted in the sunshine. I told her that it was the nicest tooth I'd ever seen. Her laugh was like a booming cannon and she let me stick my pinky finger in her green drink, which tasted like licorice.

Then it was time to get down to business.

Do you have anything of Rosemary's that I can hold for a moment? Madame asked Aunt Constance.

Aunt Constance pulled out the pearls-and-lily picture of my mother.

Will this do? she asked.

Madame held the photo with both hands, closed her eyes for a minute, and then handed it back to Aunt Constance. Then we followed her into a little room inside the house, and in that room were all sorts of jars of dried herbs and things hanging from wall shelves, including animal heads and various claws. In the middle of the room stood a cutting-board table like the one Grandmother and Aunt Constance used at Windy Ridge to truss up turkeys and chickens for dinner.

Bring me a chicken, called out Madame, and a moment later a young girl who'd been working in the kitchen scurried into the room, holding a live chicken by the legs.

Madame took the chicken and put it on the board, and before we even knew what was happening, she picked up a big, shiny butcher knife and lopped off the chicken's head. Aunt Constance let out a scream and the headless chicken still kicked around for a minute. Mrs. Foxworth just quietly sipped her green drink and didn't say anything, as if this was the most casual thing in the world. And I stood there wishing that Belfry was here to see this, because I knew that when I told him about it someday, he'd probably say that I was fibbing because no one back at home invited you over for refreshments and then lopped off the head of a chicken in front of you. Aunt Constance saw me pointing my camera at the headless chicken and she rushed over to me.

Don't you dare photograph that, she exclaimed. Go and wait for me on the front porch.

I want to see what happens, I protested, but she shoveled me out of the room before I could see anything else. Of course I hovered on the other side of the door and listened. I don't know what Madame did with that headless chicken, but this is what she said a few minutes later to Aunt Constance:

Rosemary Elizabeth Lancaster was indeed here in this town, but the spirits tell me that she left some weeks ago. Like the early adventurers determined to discover the soul of this country and discover the secrets of their own souls at the same time, Rosemary has gone out west.

Where out west? asked Aunt Constance.

California, Madame told her. San Francisco, to be exact. Like so many other young souls today.

The hippies are flocking there in droves, Mrs. Foxworth chimed in. You hear about it on the news all the time.

Madame went on:

However, if you follow Rosemary out there, you will not find her. You will see her, yes, but you won't find Rosemary Elizabeth Lancaster.

This is very confusing, said Aunt Constance, and I immediately remembered what the tarot cards had told Moody and Bun when I asked if we would find my mother, and the cards said yes and no at the same time. Everyone in New Orleans seemed to be telling us the same thing. But what did it mean? This all felt like an odd wild-goose chase to me, and my mother felt farther away than ever. I started to think that the only place she really lived now was in the pearls-and-lily picture.

To be clear, are you telling us not to follow Rosemary? pressed Aunt Constance.

Not at all, said Madame. You should certainly follow her. Because you will also find the real Rosemary Elizabeth Lancaster if you do so. That is, you'll find Julia's real mother.

But Rosemary *is* Julia's mother, Aunt Constance said, her voice rising. I should know—I was there when Julia was born.

I couldn't stand it anymore and opened the door a crack and peeked in. Madame was smiling gently and after that she wouldn't say anything else. But she chopped off one of the chicken's feet, wrapped it in a red silk pocket square, and handed it to Aunt Constance.

Keep this with you at all times on your journey, Madame said. It will lead you to Rosemary and guard you on your journey.

I could hardly believe it, but Aunt Constance actually took the chicken foot and tucked it into her basket purse, which up to that point had only held things like rose-smelling talcum powder and a tapestry coin purse and weekly church programs. Now there was a chicken foot in there given to her by New Orleans's most famous voodoo queen, who had a gold tooth and drank burning green potions the way other people drink water.

Belfry would simply never believe it.

PART THREE
Out West

CHAPTER EIGHT

World's End

I suppose that the sky is the sky wherever you go. I never paid much attention to it back at Windy Ridge, unless the sun was blazing too hot up there or if there were big black thunderclouds in it. In other words, unless there was something exciting happening in that slice of sky that just happened to live over our patch of land along the Hudson River in New York.

But when you're in Texas, the sky is different. There is so much of it that you get lost in it even when you're still on the ground.

I hate the Texas sky, Aunt Constance said.

I was surprised when she told me this because Aunt Constance didn't usually say her opinions out loud. Lancasters did not broadcast their opinions. To do so was common and coarse. But lately she'd been telling me more and more of her thoughts about things, and it was like seeing the inside of a house that has always been closed up and wreathed in ivy before. I was discovering all of the house's rooms and furniture and books and wallpaper.

This sky is so gray and huge and it makes me feel too small, Aunt Constance went on as we drove through the Texas countryside.

And even the land is so flat and hard and mean-looking, she added. I miss the Windy Ridge lawns and roses and oak trees. I'm dying to see green again.

I felt bad for Aunt Constance that she hated both the Texas sky and the Texas land so much, because Texas was a very big state and you had to drive for a very long time to get through it, and we needed to get through it to reach California. I didn't mind Texas as much as she did, because we got to stay in dusty little motels as we went and sometimes the owners would have a television there. We never had a television at Windy Ridge, and I liked to sneak looks at all of those flat people living strange lives inside that electronic box.

But then one day we got to a part of northwestern Texas where there were no little motels at all. Aunt Constance drove and drove and it started to get dark, but we found no place to stay for the night.

I don't see that we have a choice: we'll just have to camp out in the desert, Aunt Constance told me, and I thought about how different she seemed ever since we went to Paw Paw and she wouldn't even think about sleeping in a teepee.

She drove off the road and parked in the middle of the dry plain. We pulled our Oriental carpets out to use as sleeping mats, and I took out the silver candlesticks also, to help make Aunt Constance feel at home. But it was too windy for the candles to stay lit, and it got very cold out there in the desert night. Luckily Aunt Constance had brought along a mink coat and a beaver coat and we could sleep under those.

Isn't it funny? said Aunt Constance. Grandmother used to wear these fur coats to the Colony Club and fancy dinners in the city. If only she could see us now, huddled under her fine furs like hoboes on the ground.

I told her that I didn't think that many hoboes had fine mink coats, but she was already fast asleep by then, the fur ruffling in the desert wind.

The next morning for breakfast we had peanut butter spread on crackers, and my stomach was still growling when we got back into the car and started driving into all of that nothingness again. I turned on the car radio but we got only static, and Aunt Constance said this was the sort of country that made you go crazy. So we were pretty happy when we saw a sign in the middle of that desert:

Aunt Constance stopped the car in front of the sign, and we got out and studied it together.

How puzzling, said Aunt Constance. I can't tell if Mr. Cantor-Battle would shoot us if we drove up to the house or welcome us with a bunch of daisies.

I said that it sounded like some sort of riddle. We stood there and puzzled some more, and the wind blew swirls of dust around us. And then Aunt Constance said that she'd take her chances; she couldn't stand one more night out in the Texas desert. She rummaged around in one of our trunks and pulled out a white lace handkerchief with the initials *EL* sewn onto it, which stood for *Ellen Lancaster*. That was Grandmother's name, and the handkerchief had belonged to her. Then Aunt Constance tied the handkerchief around the end of a stick like a flag, and we got back into the car and drove onto the World's End Cattle Ranch, with Aunt Constance waving the flag out her window as we hummed along.

A white flag is a universal sign of surrender, she explained. No one with a scrap of manners would dare to shoot two ladies waving an embroidered white lace flag.

Then she added that someone with a name like the Honorable Winston Cantor-Battle simply must have at least a scrap of manners, and I hoped for our sake that she was right.

On the horizon stood a long, low house, and when we got closer, we saw a man standing on the front porch. He wore tan trousers that looked like balloons tucked into his high leather boots; a little round monocle glimmered over his right eye; and his hair shone like it had been combed through with butter. A horsewhip dangled from his left hand, and I told Aunt Constance to turn around quick: he probably had a pistol in his back pocket. But then he waved at us, and Aunt Constance pulled up in front of him and got out of the car.

Good afternoon, sir, she said. My name is Constance Lancaster of Windy Ridge, New York. Are you the Honorable Winston Cantor-Battle?

To the best of my knowledge, he replied.

We are terribly sorry to intrude, Aunt Constance said meekly, but my niece, Julia Lancaster, and I are on a long journey through the state and are hoping to board here for the night.

There is indeed plenty of room here at World's End, the Honorable Winston Cantor-Battle told Aunt Constance, but then he didn't say another word after that. There was an awkward silence until I piped up.

How can you tell the difference between a trespasser and a traveler? I asked him.

It's simple, said the Honorable Winston Cantor-Battle. Trespassers don't ask permission to be here, and travelers do. Trespassers are sullen and quiet, and travelers always have fine stories to tell. Trespassers are squirrelly hiders, and travelers are curious adventurers.

After this little speech, he lit a pipe, blew out a cloud of smoke, and asked what brought us all the way out to western Texas. Before Aunt Constance could respond, I blurted out that we were looking for my hippie mother, who'd run away to Greenwich Village and then gone to New Orleans to learn voodoo, but that the city's voodoo queen had given Aunt Constance a magic chicken foot and told us to go to California to find my mother, who had flocked there with legions of other hippies.

The Honorable Winston Cantor-Battle just stared at me for a minute, his eyeglass glinting in the sunset. Then he told us:

You clearly meet all of the criteria of travelers and not trespassers. Welcome to World's End. Please join me for supper, and stay as my guests overnight at the ranch.

Right away we noticed two unusual things about World's End.

First: every bit of the floor and the walls was covered in animal hides—some with the heads still on them. They included:

- *2 bears (one black and one brown)*
- *1 cheetah*
- *1 leopard*
- *2 zebras*
- *1 lion*
- *1 lioness*

There were cows too, of course, because this was a cattle ranch after all. The Honorable Winston Cantor-Battle informed us that he had shot every single one of these animals himself.

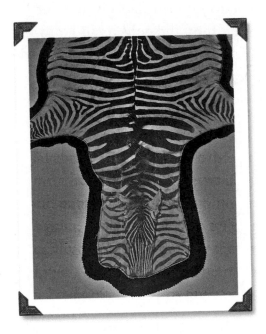

The second unusual thing: all of the ranch servants and cattle hands were Chinese. I had only seen a Chinese person once when we lived at Windy Ridge: a woman who got lost on her way to New York City and stopped her car near the five-and-dime to ask Belfry and me directions.

But at World's End even the cowboys had come all the way from a farm in China's countryside, where the

Honorable Winston Cantor-Battle had lived long ago. I couldn't stop looking at them. I immediately pulled out my postcards and wrote one to Belfry, another to Jack in Paw Paw, and a third one to Moody and Bun to tell them about it.

That night dinner was served in a big room with walls covered with moose heads. We ate big steaks that practically took up a whole plate each, and a fire roared at the far end of the room in a big stone fireplace.

Do you ever feel bad when you shoot animals? I asked the Honorable Winston Cantor-Battle.

Never, he told me. If I hadn't shot these divine creatures, they'd have died someday anyway. There would have been nothing left of them, no record that they'd ever even existed. But this way, they'll live on in posterity here at World's End.

I'd never looked at it this way before, but those moose heads still made me feel funny.

I would feel bad shooting a zebra, I told him. They're so pretty.

Haven't you ever been hunting? he asked me.

You mean with a gun? I asked him.

Lancasters have not borne arms since the Revolutionary War, Aunt Constance interrupted. She added: And anyway, Grandmother Lancaster did not approve of ladies bearing guns—even small pistols. It's not very feminine.

Nonsense, said the Honorable Winston Cantor-Battle, and informed us: All Texan women can shoot guns. It's as much a ladies' pastime as drinking tea. Plus, it's just good common sense to have one with you at all times. You might have to kill a rattler at any moment—or worse, a trespasser with no good stories to tell.

And—he went on—anyone who consents to eat a steak or any other sort of meat should know what it feels like to kill the animal from which it came.

With that, he beckoned to a young Chinese servant who'd been standing quietly in the corner.

This is Li Yong, said the Honorable Winston Cantor-Battle, and told us firmly: Tomorrow morning he will take both of you hunting on the ranch grounds.

Oh, we really couldn't trouble you, exclaimed Aunt Constance.

I won't hear a word of protest, said the Honorable Winston Cantor-Battle. This is what the best sort of travelers do—they have new experiences. And now you'll have one more adventure story to tell your next host. You'll be in good hands with Li Yong. He's an expert marksman.

Li Yong bowed silently. Aunt Constance didn't know what to say, but I noticed that she didn't eat any more of her steak.

• • •

Just before dawn, there was a knock on our door. There on the other side stood Li Yong with three shotguns. He looked at our flowered dresses, left the room, and came back with an armful of clothes.

You cannot wear ladies' clothes, he told us. You need man clothes. Like pants and tall boots to protect from scorpions and snakes.

Aunt Constance looked like she might cry but she put on the clothes anyway. Then she popped on her flowery straw hat, tucked her lace handkerchief into her pocket, and picked up her basket purse, which she hugged to her chest.

We may be going into the wilderness, Julia, but let's not be totally uncivilized, she said.

I put my camera around my neck and we set off. The sun rose over the horizon just as we walked out of the house. Rabbits and gophers scattered through the dry brush as we walked across the plain.

We will go into the canyon, Li Yong told us. The animals flock there to drink, and there is always good hunting.

The land got rocky and then very steep and from the grass we heard rattles but didn't see any snakes, which was good because Aunt Constance and I both hated snakes. After a while, we came to a rocky hill that led down to a stream. We settled behind some boulders overlooking the water and then had to sit very quiet and still so the animals wouldn't hear us.

Soon a very strange-looking pig with bristles all over his body stumped down to the water.

It is a javelina, Li Yong whispered to Aunt Constance. Point the gun at his heart.

Aunt Constance pointed her gun but her hands were shaking.

I can't do it, she told Li Yong.

Yes, you can—just pull the trigger, said Li Yong.

No, I can't, said Aunt Constance, and she threw the gun down on the boulder. Suddenly the gun went off and the bullet must have hit the stone cliff just above the javelina, because a big rock chipped off it and landed right on top of the animal. Li Yong leaped up from our hiding place and scrambled down to the pig's side.

You got him, lady, he yelled to Aunt Constance.

Ohhhhhhh, wailed Aunt Constance. The poor dear. I feel simply terrible. Hopefully the ranch cook can make something from him, perhaps a pork pâté or a tasty terrine.

Li Yong dragged the javelina back to our hiding spot. It was awful to see the animal squashed and dead like that. Just then several more javelina trotted down the cliff to the stream. They sniffed the ground so hard I thought that they'd cut up their snouts on those rocks. Li Yong seemed very surprised.

You must have hunting magic, he told Aunt Constance. So many javelina. Usually only one or two come down here in a day.

Now four or five more of the pigs appeared over the cliff and came down to the stream—and then three more. They all sniffed the air and the ground like they were looking for something that they wanted to find very badly. Then they started to march toward us.

This is not good, said Li Yong. When javelina are by themselves, they are easy to shoot. But when they are in a big pack, they can be dangerous. Get behind me.

What can they be looking for? wondered Aunt Constance. Five more javelina came over the cliff to join the herd.

What if they smell that chicken foot from Madame Flavie Batilde? I asked. Is it in your basket?

Aunt Constance went white.

That must be it, she said, and then at that moment the pigs began to thunder toward us.

Li Yong picked up a gun and shot in their direction. One of the javelina fell but the rest kept coming.

Run! Li Yong hollered, and all three of us started to scramble back toward the house as fast as we could. The pigs ran after us, kicking up a big dust cloud as they went.

Give them the chicken foot, I yelled to Aunt Constance, but she gripped her basket purse closer to her chest. Her straw hat flew off her head and got ripped to shreds under the hooves of the running pigs.

As the ranch came into sight, the Honorable Winston Cantor-Battle ran out onto the porch with a big gun and he began shooting at the javelina. A few more of them fell, and the bullets that didn't hit the pigs made explosions in the dusty ground all around us. We finally clattered up the back stairs of the house; Aunt Constance ran straight through the ranch house, into our room, and slammed the door. She lay gasping for breath on her bed, still hugging the purse to her chest, and for a while we didn't say anything to each other.

But when she caught her breath and could talk again, she turned to me and said:

I may not be the most worldly person, Julia, but even *I* know better than to throw a gift from a voodoo queen to a gaggle of wild pigs.

This, of course, made all the sense in the world, and for the first time since we left Windy Ridge, I realized that Aunt Constance was very brave in her own way.

That night a full moon rose over the plains, and the light made everything in Texas look ghostly and blue. Li Yong and some of the other ranch hands had fetched the dead javelina—including the one that got squashed by the rock Aunt Constance shot off the cliff—and brought the animals to the ranch cook, who made a fine big steaming barbecue out of them, smoking the meat in a fire pit dug into the ground. It was a hot night, so we ate the barbecue out on the back porch and listened to the cows lowing out on the plains.

One of the cowboys brought a Chinese instrument with lots of strings up onto the porch and began to play a quiet song that made me feel strange, but the Honorable Winston Cantor-Battle seemed to be enjoying it so much that he practically melted into the porch.

I love this country, he told Aunt Constance and me. He took a big puff on his pipe and went on:

Here we are, in the Lone Star State, with the big moon above and all of the space and air in the world. You can be whoever you want out here.

I'm telling you, ladies, he added, when you find the place where you belong, a place that makes you feel like the best version of yourself, you stay put. Never, ever let it go. Never leave it. Because once you're away from it, you're not your whole self anymore.

I know exactly what you mean, said Aunt Constance. She looked sadly at the horizon, and I knew that she must be thinking of Windy Ridge, where Lancasters had felt the most like themselves for hundreds of years before it got sold to Tipsy Lipps.

One of the cowboys came up to the porch out of the blue night and whispered something to the Honorable Winston Cantor-Battle, who smiled around his pipe. Smoke swirled around his face as he turned to Aunt Constance and me.

Three new calves were born into our herd tonight, he

told us. That's the most in a long time. So it appears that you are not two travelers, but three: Constance Lancaster, Julia Lancaster, and Lady Luck.

We all walked out onto the moonlit field to see the baby cows. Even though they were less than an hour old, they already stood up on their own, wobbling and glistening out there in the middle of all of the World's End nothingness that made the Honorable Winston Cantor-Battle feel so much like himself, that nothingness that was filled with dust and heat and sad music brought along from the other side of the world.

CHAPTER NINE

Ghost Town

Here are some of the big things that happened after we left World's End:

1. I found a big passel of Indian beads near the Fort Apache Indian Reservation in Arizona that I made into a necklace so long that it almost reached my toes:

2. Aunt Constance and I had a picnic on the edge of the Grand Canyon, and a big wooden box of our Lancaster silverware fell over the side and bounced hundreds of feet down the canyon walls into the Colorado River, which was emerald green that day.

3. We stayed overnight in Las Vegas and had dinner at a fancy casino. Afterward Aunt Constance decided to play a hand of bridge at one of the gambling card tables and lost a lot of money. Then she cried and said that we'd have to sell off even more of our Windy Ridge things to pay for the money she lost to the casino, but someone told her to try again, which she did, and this time she won the bridge game and also got back a little bit more money than she lost, so we came out ahead. I said that the Madame Batilde chicken foot was giving us good luck, which was a good sign that it was going to help us find my mother when we got to San Francisco. Aunt Constance said that Las Vegas was more crooked than any of those voodoo salons in New Orleans's French Quarter, and we drove out of town in a hurry. In fact, we skittered out of Las Vegas so fast that Aunt Constance forgot to fill up the gas

can for the car. And when you're driving out there in the middle of nowhere, you need three things:

1. Food;
2. Water;
3. Gas for the car—so you don't get stranded in the desert with all of that tumbleweed.

Which is exactly what happened to us. The needle on the dashboard pointed at the *E* for *empty,* and soon the car started going slower and slower even when Aunt Constance pushed down hard with her foot on the gas pedal, and then it stopped altogether.

What are we going to do? I asked her.

We'll have to wait for someone to drive down the highway and then ask them for a ride to the next gas station, Aunt Constance told me unhappily, and added: I'm sorry that I was so careless, Julia.

So we got out of the car and sat on the front bumper. An hour went by, and nobody came down the highway. Then another hour went by, and the sun got so hot that it started to make us dizzy. So we dragged two of our trunks out of the car, stood them on their sides, and put an Oriental carpet over them to make a little sun tent.

And we sat inside the hutch and ate some cookies and played gin rummy to kill time, and even though Aunt Constance was very upset about being stranded in the hot desert, she still had enough of her wits about her to beat me at almost every hand.

We Lancaster women have been shrewd card players for at least six generations—even when under duress, she told me.

Late that afternoon, I saw a flicker of movement way down the road, and we both scrambled out of the hutch and stood with our hands shielding our eyes from the sun's glare, and soon the flicker turned out to be a rusty Ford pickup truck that had probably once been red and now was almost no color at all. The driver stopped the truck next to our trunk-and-carpet hutch. He wore a cowboy hat and a star badge on his vest.

Hop in and I'll take you to the next town for gas, he told us.

How far is the next town? fussed Aunt Constance. She was worried about leaving all of our Windy Ridge things alone in the car for too long.

It's only thirty miles north of here, said the man. It's called Gold Point, Nevada.

Aunt Constance peered down at our map. Where is it? she asked. I don't see a Gold Point anywhere on the map.

That's because it doesn't exist, the man told her.

Aunt Constance looked bewildered.

What on earth do you mean? she asked him.

Well, it existed once upon a time, the man in the cowboy hat explained. It was a mining town about a hundred years ago, when there was still gold in the hills. But now the gold is gone, and so are most of the people. Gold Point's considered a ghost town and so the state took it off all the maps.

I can assure you, though, he added, that the town is still very much around. I'm the sheriff, after all. My name is Sheriff Stone.

So, with that, Aunt Constance and I climbed up into his truck to take a ride to nowhere.

How did you become sheriff of a town that doesn't exist? I asked him.

No one else wanted the job, said Sheriff Stone. So I

held an election and—what do you know?—I won hands down. There were three voters in total: me, myself, and I.

You also happen to be looking at the town's mayor, fire chief, and reverend, he added.

That sounds like a lot of responsibility, Aunt Constance said.

Well, I thought it was my duty, Sheriff Stone told us, and then he pointed up at the hills.

There's Gold Point now, he told us.

Aunt Constance and I leaned forward and squinted, but we couldn't make out a thing. If there was a town up there, it sure blended into the hills, like a chameleon blends into a tree branch. Sheriff Stone turned his truck off the road; we drove straight into the desert and ran over a lot of dry plants and we got bumped around a lot as he plowed up into the hills.

And soon the buildings of Gold Point came out of the background like magic.

This is Main Street, Sheriff Stone told us.

I can tell you right now that Gold Point's Main Street looked nothing like any other Main Street I'd ever seen. It made Paw Paw's Main Street look fancy. First of all, there were no grocery stores, no gas stations, no ice cream parlors. What there was instead: maybe ten old buildings cobbled together from wood planks, and at least half of them were falling down or looked like they were sinking deep into the dusty ground.

Tumbleweed did cartwheels across the street in the wind. A rusted-out car languished in an empty lot, its front doors covered in bullet holes.

That's where I do my target practice, explained Sheriff Stone, and he stopped the car. Hop out, ladies. I'll run back to my garage and get you-all a canister of gasoline.

He ambled over to a falling-down shack and disappeared inside.

Aunt Constance wrapped her arms around herself and peered around.

I've never seen such a lonely place before, she told me. It's the loneliest place in the world. I can't wait to get back into our car and drive away as fast as we can—

And the next thing I knew, she was lying on the ground. Aunt Constance had accidentally stepped in a hole in the ground and sprained her ankle.

We got stuck at Gold Point—the loneliest place in the world—for a whole week.

Sheriff Stone was not only Gold Point's policeman, mayor, fire chief, and reverend; his house was also the town restaurant and he was its chef. He made breakfast each day for all of us, and it was usually a hill of bacon the size of a haystack that he cooked over a fire out in the backyard. There was no running water out there, and Sheriff Stone got all of his water from barrels that collected rainwater:

I fill the others up with tap water when I drive down to Las Vegas every few weeks, he told me. That's where I was coming from when I picked up you-all.

Aunt Constance and I slept in Sheriff Stone's house, which also served as Gold Point's jail. Years ago, lots of drunken gold miners had gotten locked up in those jail cells, Sheriff Stone told us. But now Aunt Constance and I had taken up residence in them instead, sleeping on cell cots. I thought it was all very exciting and pretended that I was in a Wild West movie. Aunt Constance, on the other hand, said it was the most demoralizing experience of her life and that Grandmother Lancaster was going to hurl a lightning bolt down at us from heaven, and then she even said, "Curse you, Rosemary," because my mother was the reason we were stuck here in the first place.

Anyway, on our first morning there, after we'd eaten the breakfast bacon, Sheriff Stone said that we should probably go get our car off the highway.

How can we do that? asked Aunt Constance crabbily. I can't drive with my foot like this. She sat on her cell cot with her bound ankle propped up on a pillow.

Julia and I will drive down and get it, he said. And she'll have to drive it back. It's too far for me to walk out there and drive it back myself.

Really? I yelled, jumping up out of my chair. Can I really drive?

Julia is a child, cried Aunt Constance. She can't drive a car. That's ridiculous.

Oh, anyone with eyes, arms, and legs can drive a car, Sheriff Stone told her. And as far as I can tell, Julia has all of these things.

And then he pointed out that the only other choice was to leave the car with all of our trunks and Windy Ridge practical-travel things out there in the desert alone until Aunt Constance's ankle felt better, which might take a week or even longer.

And, he added, who knows who or what might make its way into the car and help themselves to its contents.

Aunt Constance looked stricken.

I don't see that we have a choice, then, she said. But, God in heaven, *please* go slowly.

Slow as snails, promised Sheriff Stone, and I almost died right then and there of excitement.

Sheriff Stone and I got into his truck and drove down that empty highway. I wondered if a single other person had driven down that road since we stalled there the day before.

Happily, all of our practical-travel things were still in our car. I got into the driver's seat and my heart pounded.

There's nothing to it, Sheriff Stone told me. He pointed to the floor: Here's the brake; here's the gas. Don't mix them up, and you'll be golden.

We practiced for a while until I said I thought I had the hang of it, and he got back into his truck and told me to follow him. I wished that someone would take a picture of *me* for once, because Belfry would never, ever believe this in a million years.

It was all going pretty well until I stepped too hard on the gas and the Windy Ridge car shot forward and hit the back of his truck. Not really hard, but just hard enough to make one of our travel trunks slide off the roof of my car and chunk down onto the road and break. Everything inside spilled out onto the pavement.

Why are you traveling all over creation with this crazy stuff? asked Sheriff Stone as we picked up the scattered silver and old books and some velvet curtains off the ground and piled them up in the back of his truck.

They are Windy Ridge necessities, I informed him. Our practical-travel things. Aunt Constance needs them to remind her that we are Lancasters, no matter where we are.

And what are all of these? he asked, picking up some pictures that had spilled out of a cardboard box onto the road.

That's part of my photograph collection, I said.

Can I look at them? asked Sheriff Stone.

I didn't say anything for a minute. I'd never really shown the pictures to anyone before, even Belfry. But Sheriff Stone seemed like a nice man, and he did, after all, teach me how to drive, so I told him okay, he could see the pictures.

Where're all the photos of your family? he asked,

leafing through them. He held up one of a Windy Ridge china pitcher and one of a perfectly shaped acorn that fell in our backyard last fall and one of a beetle that lived under my bed the summer before.

I don't have any family pictures, I told him.

Why not? he asked. You have hundreds of pictures of things, but no people. There has to be a reason.

I didn't look at him. Instead I started stacking the pictures into a pile.

I should mind my own beeswax, said Sheriff Stone, and he handed me back some photographs.

It's easier not to have them, I said finally.

Have what?

Pictures of people, I told him. Because then you get reminded of them. And it makes you sad.

But isn't it nice to be reminded of certain people, like family? Sheriff Stone asked.

No, it's not, I said. Because sometimes people who are supposed to stay with you forever just leave you behind instead. And so it's better not to think about them too much. That's why I like things. They don't leave, unless you move them or lose them yourself. And they always stay the same.

Sheriff Stone got a funny look on his face.

Well, that sort of makes sense, I suppose, he said. But you can't stop change from happening, you know. It comes whether you want it or not. Even with things.

He picked up a Windy Ridge silver fork from the road.

If you leave this out, it'll get tarnished, won't it?

I suppose so, I said.

And think about trees, he went on. They might live in the same place in your yard, and they'll still be there long after we're all gone, but every season and every day they look different, don't they?

That's true, I told him.

And just look at Gold Point, said Sheriff Stone. Once, hundreds of people came out here to make their fortunes. They found gold in the hills and silver too. Then one day the gold ran out, so those people all left and they took that particular American dream with them. And now that dream lives someplace else, and what's left here is a big hole in the air where that dream was, and the crumbling skeleton of a town.

So why don't you leave too? I asked him. Don't you get lonesome living in a ghost town by yourself?

Sure I do, he said. But it's my home—and it needs me. The town would disappear forever if I left. And anyway, it comforts me to be there. And we have to take comfort wherever we can find it, don't you think?

Suddenly I thought of Aunt Constance when he said this. Before we left Windy Ridge, I never thought of Aunt Constance as being comforting. Grandmother wasn't a comfort either, and neither was my mother—even before she left to be a hippie full-time. I got my comfort instead from the house and the gardens and my tree swing and from Belfry.

But out here, on this car trip, with the house and gardens and Belfry gone, I realized that Aunt Constance had become my comfort. And our dusty car with our practical-travel things inside had become our Windy Ridge. When I realized this, I felt better than I'd felt for a long time—steady and cozy.

Sheriff Stone and I picked up the rest of my photographs, and then we got into the cars and made our way slowly back into Gold Point. And I didn't even drive our Windy Ridge car into the back of his truck again even once.

I learned two other useful skills while Aunt Constance and I lived as honorary citizens of Gold Point, Nevada, eating bacon with Sheriff Stone and waiting for Aunt Constance's ankle to get better.

1. How to use a pistol. One afternoon it got very hot and no wind blew through the town for a change, and there was absolutely nothing to do at all. So Sheriff Stone and I sat on the porch of the building that had once been Gold Point's saloon, which stood across the street from the old rusted-out car, and Sheriff Stone shot a few times at the car's front door, which was the

main target. Then he let me shoot it once, and the gun made my whole body shake, and even though I hit the door right in the middle, I gave him the gun back right away. After that, Sheriff Stone called me Deadeye and told me that I was his official deputy sheriff.

2. How to mine for gold. Sheriff Stone gave me a hammer and a chisel, and for a few hours I went out into the hills and chipped away at the rocky faces of the hills. At first I didn't find anything but gray old rocks. Just when I was about to give up, a big hunk of gray rock fell away from the hill and underneath was a big, fat, shiny piece of gold. I hacked it out and ran down the hill, whooping like an Indian. Sheriff Stone lumbered off the saloon porch, and Aunt Constance hobbled to the door of the jailhouse to see what I was hollering about.

Look, look, I yelled, and told them: I found gold, a huge piece of it, as big as my head almost! Maybe this means that the miners and the American dream will come back to Gold Point again, and you won't have to be lonely anymore, Sheriff Stone. And, Aunt Constance—now the Lancasters can be rich again, and we can maybe even get Windy Ridge back.

Sheriff Stone picked up my hunk of gold and turned it from side to side.

Honey, he said. I don't know how to tell you this, but this ain't gold. It's pyrite.

Oh, I said, and stood very still. What's pyrite?

Well, it's what they call fool's gold, he said. Looks like the real thing enough to fool even an expert. I'm so sorry to burst your bubble.

I just stood there and didn't say anything. Aunt Constance reached out and petted my hair quietly. Sheriff Stone put my big hunk of fool's gold down on the porch.

Look at the bright side, Deadeye, he told me. Now you have a fancy doorstop to add to your practical-travel things in those trunks of yours.

CHAPTER TEN

Pinkham's Hotel
for Ladies

Usually when we were driving away from the middle of nowhere and toward civilization, as Aunt Constance called it, she would get in a better mood. Sometimes she was in good enough a mood to let me listen to the car radio—as long as it was the Beatles singing and not what she called "that dreadful Janis Joplin creature."

But this time, as we drove across the Nevada desert away from Gold Point and into California and up toward San Francisco, Aunt Constance's mood got worse, not better. She seemed very nervous and she didn't talk a lot, and most of the time her mouth made a very straight line.

What's San Francisco like? I asked her as we got closer to the city.

I've never been there, said Aunt Constance, looking straight ahead. But it's supposed to be very pretty. Lots of good families have lived there over the years.

Why are all of the hippies going to San Francisco, Aunt Constance? I asked her.

I don't know, she answered. They just are.

How many of them are there? I pressed. Will the men have Jesus hair like the ones in New York? Will the lady hippies be wearing any clothes?

Oh, Julia, please stop pestering me right now—just let me concentrate on my driving, said Aunt Constance, gripping the steering wheel very tight.

I didn't know what to do then. Aunt Constance was never short with me like this and it hurt my feelings. I hoped she'd be nice again when we got into the city and she felt more at home from being near restaurants and hotels and churches again.

Soon we drove past this sign:

Aunt Constance drove us straight to an inexpensive but respectable place called Pinkham's Hotel for Ladies. They gave us a room with a deep bathtub that had claws for feet, and a big bed with a lace canopy over it. Downstairs in the hotel there was a card-playing parlor and a pink tearoom, and everything was terribly ladylike.

I thought this would make Aunt Constance happy, but she didn't even really glance at any of these things. She didn't seem to be seeing out of her own eyes. Her nervousness made me nervous inside too. She had a hotel maid wash and press her long flowered dress, and then she went out and bought a new straw hat with daisies on it.

Now I look like myself again, she said, looking at herself in the mirror.

But I didn't think that she looked like she used to look at Windy Ridge. Something had changed about her. I didn't know what exactly. I wondered if I seemed different and looked different too. I stood next to her in the mirror and frowned at myself.

What is it, Julia? Aunt Constance asked, glancing at me.

Do you think we look alike? I asked her.

A little bit, she said. You can certainly tell that we're both Lancasters, from our eyes and the shape of our noses.

I peered closer at my face in the reflection.

Do you think I look like my mother? I asked.

Aunt Constance walked away from the mirror. She picked up her basket purse.

Julia, I'm going out for the rest of the day, she told me. You are to stay right here at the hotel and wait for me to return.

But why can't I come along? I asked her. I got to come with you almost everywhere else. Like the voodoo parlors in New Orleans and out shooting javelina at World's End.

It's different this time, she told me.

How? I asked her.

Because this time I truly feel that your mother is close by, said Aunt Constance.

This didn't make any sense to me.

But we thought she was probably close by in New York, and New Orleans too, I said. And you wanted me to be with you and to see her then—so why not now?

Please don't be rebellious, said Aunt Constance, her voice rising. Especially now, of all times—when I truly need you to be good.

But I don't want to sit here and play cards and drink tea with all of these old ladies, I told her.

Enough, Julia, said Aunt Constance.

I want to see my mother, I yelled.

Oh, for God's sake—stop it! Aunt Constance shouted back at me.

My mouth fell open. Aunt Constance never lost her temper. Only vulgar people lost their temper, especially with children. Certainly not Lancasters. Definitely not

Aunt Constance. I expected her to collect herself and tell me that she was sorry but instead she walked to the door.

I mean it, Joooooolia, she told me in a steely voice. Do not move from this hotel. I'll be back soon.

As she left the room, I heard her ask a bellboy for directions to someplace called Hate Ashbury, and then she left, her long flowered dress flowing out behind her.

I just stood there for a few minutes after she left. The new, steady, comfy feeling was gone. The old cloud-over-sun feeling came back. And now I was afraid, on top of everything else. Why did Aunt Constance want me not to see my mother all of a sudden?

I crawled into bed and pulled the covers over my head.

One day turned into two days, and two into three. I obeyed Aunt Constance and hung around Pinkham's Hotel for Ladies while she went off each day to Hate Ashbury. We didn't talk to each other much at breakfast or dinner, and Aunt Constance got more nervous and steelier than ever. By the fourth day, I had read the hotel's copy of *Reader's Digest* about a million times and had written three post-cards each to Belfry, Jack, Mrs. Foxworth, Moody and Bun, the Honorable Winston Cantor-Battle, and Sheriff Stone. I took so many pictures of the resident terrier—a gummy-eyed old thing—that I ran out of my last batch of film for my camera.

And then I finally got fed up and decided that if I was old enough to be a deputy sheriff and shoot a pistol, then I was old enough to take a short walk by myself. Aunt Constance didn't have to know, I told myself, and what she didn't know couldn't get her mad.

I strolled out into Union Square and found a drugstore where I could buy some more postcards and film. There was a food counter there and I had enough money for a chocolate egg cream in addition to the film and cards, so I sat down on a stool at the food counter and ordered one. A little television sat behind the counter:

I asked the old waitress with tall, dyed-black hair if I could watch it. She turned the television on, and since there was no one else but me at the counter, she clumped down to the far end of the drugstore and began buffing her nails, leaving me to watch television by myself.

At first there was a show on about a masked cowboy called the Lone Ranger, who liked to shout, "Hi-yo, Silver—away!" and then there would be a horse chase and lots of yelling and carrying on. It was a dumb show, but it was nice to watch it and not think about Aunt Constance and my missing-but-close-by mother, and I was sorry when it was over and my egg cream was gone.

Then the news came on. No one ever watched the news at Windy Ridge. Grandmother said that television newsmen were hysteria-mongers, whatever that meant. I had never seen a hysteria-monger before, so of course I stayed right there on my stool and kept watching. The newsman talked about the war in Vietnam, which he said was getting very bad. And then he talked about how the war was making many people across the country really mad, and there were pictures of those angry people out in the streets protesting. And a lot of them looked like those hippies back in the Greenwich Village park, who carried signs that said things like, *Make love, not war.*

Just then the waitress came over and turned down the television's volume and looked at me.

You allowed to be watching the news? she asked, and not in a nice way.

Oh yes, ma'am, I said with my best Lancaster manners, and added: My grandmother says it's very important to be apprised of current events, so you can be conversational at soirées.

I hoped this fell into the category of white lie instead of just plain old lie. The waitress looked at me like I'd spoken to her in Japanese. She shut the television off anyway.

It's giving me a headache, all the news about the war, she told me, and popped a piece of gum into her mouth. This country's going straight down the toilet, she added. Why can't things just go back to the way they were? I hate all of these hippies, each and every one of them. They make me sick, I tell you. The cops oughta go clean 'em all outta the Haight.

This rang a bell. Wasn't Aunt Constance going to a place called the Hate every day? Maybe they were the same place.

What is the Hate? I asked the waitress as innocently as possible.

Haight-Ashbury, the waitress told me, is the neighborhood where all of those hippie degenerates go and lie around like a bunch of dead cats and generally waste their lives. They're all worryin' their families sick. No good will come of it, I tell you. Young people today got no sense of duty or manners, not at all.

I had many more questions, but it was getting late and Aunt Constance would be getting back soon. So I thanked the waitress for the information and marched back to the hotel.

Well, the moment I walked into Pinkham's Hotel for Ladies, I wished that I'd stayed back at the drugstore, because Aunt Constance was waiting for me right there in the lobby, her face as red as a cooked lobster. She swooped over to me and grabbed me by the shoulder and marched me into the card-playing parlor.

Where *were* you? she cried. I've been worried sick, Julia—sick!

I went out to buy some film and postcards, I told her, and showed her my drugstore bag.

Aunt Constance burst into tears and buried her face in her hands. I didn't know what to do, so I just stood there with my film and postcards and waited for a long time for her to take her hands away from her face. Two old ladies came into the parlor, took one look at Aunt Constance, and wobbled back out again as quickly as their rickety old legs could carry them. Finally Aunt Constance took a few long, shuddery breaths and moved her hands away from her face.

Sit down, Julia, she said, wiping her eyes with the backs of her hands. I have something to tell you.

I sat down, my heart pounding.

What is it? I asked.

I found Rosemary today, she said in a trembling voice. I found your mother.

The cloud-over-sun came back again, and this time it was a black cloud, a thundercloud, even.

Where? I heard myself ask.

Aunt Constance stared at her shaking hands.

A neighborhood named Haight-Ashbury, she told me. And she's living there in something called a commune. That means a house with a lot of different people living together.

Like a hotel? I asked.

No, said Aunt Constance after a long pause. Not at all like a hotel.

Julia, she went on, my instincts were right. I've decided that you are not to see her after all.

How come? I cried.

She's not exactly . . . herself, Aunt Constance said carefully, and suddenly I remembered what Madame Batilde had told her back in New Orleans.

You will see her, yes, but you won't find Rosemary Elizabeth Lancaster.

And what's more: she is going to be staying here in California, said Aunt Constance, trying hard not to cry again. And live with all of those terrible hippie people in that commune, instead of coming back to her own family. So, tonight we're going to pack up our things. We're leaving first thing tomorrow morning.

Does she know that I'm here too? I asked.

Yes, said Aunt Constance.

I'm not leaving tomorrow—not until I see her too, I told her.

I'm sorry, Julia, but that's not going to be possible, said Aunt Constance. You have to believe that I have your best interest at heart.

I'm not a baby anymore, I yelled. Where is she?

Aunt Constance stood up.

I'm going to tell the front desk that we're checking out. Please go upstairs and start getting your things in order.

She left the room.

I sat there by myself and felt like I had an angry swarm of bees buzzing in my head and stomach. This whole long trip with our practical-travel things had seemed sort of like a strange dream. But now that my mother was found, the trip stopped feeling like a dream. I wanted to see Rosemary Elizabeth Lancaster. I wanted to see her, whether she was acting like herself or not. I wanted to see if I looked like her and to see why she wanted to live out here in a strange place with strangers instead of at home with her sister and her daughter, in the house where her family had lived for hundreds of years.

And to ask her why she hadn't wanted me.

Just then I noticed that Aunt Constance had left her

basket purse on the table, and there was a slip of paper inside. I reached over and pulled it out. On that piece of paper, in her handwriting, appeared this address:

1468 Haight Street

I still cannot believe what I did next.

I took the paper and a five-dollar bill from her basket purse, and then I snuck out of the lobby while Aunt Constance's back was turned.

Then I was out on the street, and I got into the backseat of a taxi and slammed the door shut behind me.

Please take me here, sir, I told the driver, and gave him the slip of paper.

CHAPTER ELEVEN

1468 Haight Street

The taxi driver dropped me off on a corner. I looked up and the street signs read HAIGHT STREET and ASHBURY STREET. My head swam because I knew how much trouble I would be in later for sneaking out and stealing money and disobeying, and because I was scared of what I'd find now that I was here.

There were lots of people sitting around on the street, smoking cigarettes, and the men mostly had scratchy beards and long Jesus hair like the men back in Greenwich Village, and the women all had long hair like my mother had by the time she left Windy Ridge. A lot of them were pretty dirty and I wondered if there wasn't any running water here in Haight-Ashbury, like at Jack's house in Paw Paw or Sheriff Stone's jailhouse in Gold Point.

A shaggy man who reminded me of a werewolf reached out and tugged the hem of my dress.

You got any spare change, little girl? he asked me.

I was scared of him and heard myself say, No, thank you—even though he'd asked *me* for money. Then I yanked my dress away and ran up Haight Street, looking at the house numbers until I got to a building with a small, tangled front lawn. Two women sat on the stoop, smoking one of those funny-smelling cigarettes, and one of them was playing a guitar; they had braided wilted flowers into their hair. It looked like they put those flowers in their hair a long time ago and then forgot about them.

Above the front door someone had painted the number 1468.

Excuse me, please, I called out to the women, and my voice shook.

What is it, little sister? asked one of the ladies, staring down at me.

I am looking for my mother, I told her. Her name is Rosemary Elizabeth Lancaster.

That's groovy, said the other woman. We didn't know that Rosemary had a little girl. You look exactly alike. Go on in: she's back in the kitchen, having a nap.

I climbed the front stairs and walked into the house. By now my heart was practically pounding in my throat. It sounded weird to me that my mother would be having a nap in the kitchen of all places, but everything about this place was weird. A crashing noise from the living room made me jump straight up into the air: a naked little boy stood there all by himself, just picking up a book and dropping it on the floor, over and over again. And then in the next room a man sat on the floor, playing some sort of twangy instrument that sounded to me like a cat yowling out in an alley. I realized that he wasn't wearing any clothes either, but this time Aunt Constance wasn't there to cover my eyes like she did when we saw that naked lady in Greenwich Village. I ran toward the back of the house and found myself in a grimy kitchen. A mattress lay in the middle of the floor. And on that mattress slept two women, one with her back to me. She had orangey hair like Aunt Constance, but she looked too skinny to be my mother.

Mother, I called out.

The woman didn't stir. I walked over and gave her shoulder a little shake.

Mother, is that you? I said.

The woman moved a little and sat up very slowly and groaned, her hair covering her face. She moved the curtain of hair away and stared at me with half-opened eyes. Then she gave a little smile.

Well, hello, Julia, she said, and her voice sounded like it had gravel in it. Where did you come from?

I didn't move a muscle.

Is Constance with you too? my mother asked blearily, looking over my shoulder.

I'm by myself, I told her.

Good, she said. My head is pounding. I couldn't handle Constance right now. What time is it?

It's five o'clock, I said, still not moving an inch.

In the morning or afternoon? she yawned.

It seemed pretty obvious to me that it was in the afternoon and I started to get mad instead of nervous.

It's daytime, Mother, I snapped.

She stretched and patted the mattress next to her.

Come sit with me, she said. And call me Rosemary. I hate the word *mother*.

Why? I asked. You *are* my mother.

Mother is just so stiff, she said. And it makes me feel old. Come here, little sister. She patted the mattress.

I don't want to, I yelled. And I'm your daughter, not your sister. Aunt Constance is your sister. You're my *mother*.

She acted like she didn't even hear me. She glanced down at the other woman on the mattress, still sound asleep.

Oh, are you worried about her? my mother asked. That's Indigo. She's cool. She's just sleeping off a bad trip.

I looked hard at my mother and it really was like looking in the mirror, except her face looked oily and her eyes were puffy and she was all skin and bones and hard angles. And I realized that the last time I'd seen her was in the dining room at Windy Ridge, surrounded by our blue-and-white china and velvet curtains, and now here she was sitting on a dirty kitchen floor, looking like she'd never even heard of a bathtub. And even worse, she was acting like none of this was strange at all, like she had seen me yesterday instead of years ago. I wanted answers, and suddenly my voice sounded almost screechy when I demanded:

Why did you leave us?

Oh, you're being such a pill, she said. Don't start off by picking a fight. Come over here and sit with me for a minute. Let's just *be* together. Leave all that Windy Ridge stuff behind. Just be with me in the here and now.

I don't want to just sit there and be, I told her, my voice rising. Why are you here? Who are these people?

My mother blinked at me.

They are my family, she said.

No, they're not, I shouted. *I* am your family. And Aunt Constance too.

Well, this is my adopted family, she told me. My spiritual family. We all live together, love together, work together, and feed each other. I didn't know you'd gotten so grown-up, little sister. You should be with us here. Learn a new way of living.

Just then I heard the front door slap shut, and footsteps thundered through the house toward the kitchen. A moment later Aunt Constance almost tumbled into the room, her face bright red.

Julia—thank heavens, she cried. Come over here this instant.

Oh, stop being so hysterical, you biddy, my mother said. Then she stared at Aunt Constance's throat and narrowed her eyes.

What necklace is that? she asked, and her voice suddenly lost that fake, dreamy lilt.

The pearls Mother gave me when I graduated from Miss Horton's, said Aunt Constance, covering her neck with her hand.

They're fake, my mother snorted. You can tell that from a mile away.

Come to me, Julia, said Aunt Constance. We're leaving at once.

That's right, Constance, called my mother, standing up unsteadily. Take her back east and make her into a Barbie doll. Are you sending her to Miss Horton's when you get back? Maybe turn her into a silly, stunted old maid, like yourself?

Don't be mean to Aunt Constance, I cried.

My mother stretched her hand out to me.

Come to me, little sister, she said. You can come live with us here, and learn what life is really about.

I wouldn't live here if you paid me all the money in the world, I shouted at her suddenly. All you talk about is loving everything, but you left me behind. What kind of love is that? You'd rather be here with all of these creepy, dirty people than with us.

You know what? my mother said. You're just as uptight as poor, sad, old Constance here. You're a little, uptight Lancaster too. Go on, then. Go back to Windy Ridge. Both of you.

She lay down on the mattress again and turned her back to us.

That's it? That's all you're going to say? I yelled.

Beat it, she said, her back still turned. You're no little sister of mine.

Then I burst into tears.

I don't remember leaving that awful kitchen.

I don't remember leaving the house at 1468 Haight Street.

I don't remember getting into a taxi with Aunt Constance.

What I do remember: being in the back of that taxi with my eyes burning from crying so much, my head in Aunt Constance's lap. She was petting my hair. I remember that.

I'm sorry I did that, Aunt Constance, I said into her lap. And then I told her that she had been right, and I tried to stop crying but the tears kept coming anyway.

Aunt Constance just kept stroking my hair quietly. She didn't even scold me for disobeying and stealing and running away. Instead she looked out the window at the Haight and this strange world that we didn't belong to and where we were leaving my mother behind.

It's just you and me now, Julia, she finally said. Just the two of us. All of the other Lancasters are gone.

PART FOUR

Finding Home

CHAPTER TWELVE

Miss Horton's

The first thing that happens when you arrive at Miss Horton's School: the headmistress will sit you down and tell you how lucky you are to be there. After all, many famous ladies have gone to Miss Horton's over the last hundred years, she will say. Then she'll reel off about a dozen names that you're supposed to know but probably don't unless you sit at home reading your mother's copy of *Vogue* magazine. I doubt that my mother has been reading *Vogue* magazine out there in her dirty commune in Haight-Ashbury. Aunt Constance certainly never read it. So I barely knew anyone on the headmistress's list, but I nodded anyway and tried to look very impressed, since that's what the headmistress clearly expected.

Aunt Constance was there for that part of the talk, and while she was there, the headmistress was sugar-and-pie nice to me. I had turned twelve on our drive back from San Francisco, which meant that Miss Horton's could now take me as a student and have another Lancaster on its roster. The headmistress made a big fuss about how much she admired our family, but the moment Aunt Constance left for her hotel in New York City and drove away in our Windy Ridge car, which still had all of our practical-travel things in it, the headmistress let her smile fade away, and she turned to me and said:

I can hardly believe that you're a Lancaster. You look a little wild around the eyes to me. We clearly have our work cut out for us here.

The next thing that happens to you at Miss Horton's: they make you put away the clothes you arrived in, and then you get a uniform. There's a little plaid skirt with suspenders and a white shirt with a round collar and white socks that go up to your knees.

And after *that*, they put you in a dorm room with another girl, a stranger from Connecticut who asks to be called Muffy. Then Muffy tells you that her horse is called Mittens and that her charm bracelet has eleven charms from Tiffany & Co. on it. I told her that I was the deputy sheriff of Gold Point, a ghost town in Nevada, and that the only jewelry I owned was a pearl necklace that my hippie mother had once flung into a bush. She just looked at me funny when I said these things, and then she drew a line down the middle of our room with chalk.

Stay on your side, she warned me.

There were lots of rules to remember at Miss Horton's. You always had to be someplace at a specific time, and it was very hard for me to keep track. The headmistress gave me a schedule and there was always a bell going off, and you were supposed to run off to the next classroom or to a dining hall or to a gymnasium, where you'd have to put on another uniform and run around a field, but I was always in the wrong place at the wrong time, and most of the teachers yelled at me and told me that I was a troublemaker.

Two other things that happened when I got there:

1. They took away my Brownie camera and said they would keep it stored until the summer break. The headmistress said this was because I was making the other girls at Miss Horton's uncomfortable with all of my picture taking, but the last straw was when I took a picture of a dissected frog in our biology class to send to Jack to remind her of our frog-leg feast on the Paw Paw creek bank:

The biology teacher got upset and said that it was macabre of me to do that. I didn't know what *macabre* meant, but apparently it was bad enough that they take away your camera.

2. One night it got really hot and stuffy inside our room because it was Indian summer, and

Muffy wouldn't let me open the window, which was on her side of the chalk line, so I left the room and climbed up an ivy trellis to the dorm's roof and brought with me a bunch of postcards and a pen. I wrote a card to Belfry and one to Sheriff Stone, and it was so cool up there in the inky blackness with the stars overhead that I fell asleep. And then when I woke up, it was morning and there was a fire engine parked on the lawn below. A fireman was climbing up a ladder to the roof. He crawled over to me, picked me up, and carried me down the ladder with him, even though I told him that it was just as easy to go down the ivy trellis and offered to show him how. All of the girls from my dorm stood in a circle at the bottom of the ladder, but none of them would talk to me.

The headmistress, on the other hand, talked to me a lot that day: I had to sit in her office while she telephoned Aunt Constance, who was staying someplace in New York City called the Barbizon Hotel for Women. And when they were done talking, the headmistress told me that I could stay at Miss Horton's, but she didn't seem very happy about it. She confiscated my postcards to Belfry and Sheriff Stone.

It is utterly inappropriate for a twelve-year-old girl to be corresponding with men, she told me, and ripped the cards to shreds.

Worst of all: I couldn't find a single porch on the whole campus to sit under when I wanted to be alone. So I was stuck in that room with Muffy and her pictures of Mittens the horse and her Tiffany & Co. bracelet, and I never felt farther away from myself in my life.

There was only one thing that wasn't bad about Miss Horton's, and that was Miss Ellison. She taught English and gave us good books to read, and soon I discovered that a good book is the next best thing after a porch to hide under. You couldn't hide yourself inside a book, of course, but you could at least disappear into it in a different way, and sometimes the book would be good enough to make you forget for a few hours that you were at Miss Horton's. Miss Ellison never once called me a trouble-maker and one day she asked me to stay after class to have a talk with her.

Julia, she said. What happened to your arms? They're covered in little bruises.

I told her that some of the older girls liked to pinch me when no one else was looking.

Miss Ellison looked horrified and asked me why. I told her that I didn't know, but that the pinching had started one day after history class when we were studying Texas and the Alamo and I told the class about World's End Ranch, with all of its Chinese cowboys and javelina. Now some of the girls from the class called me a freak and a liar, and sometimes they would even leave things like bugs and worms in my bed at night.

That's awful, said Miss Ellison. Why haven't you said anything?

I told her that the headmistress hated me anyway, so there was no point. And anyway, I said, Christmas was coming in a few weeks, and I'd be going to New York City to stay with Aunt Constance at the Barbizon Hotel and the bruises would heal up then.

Come with me, Julia, said Miss Ellison, and for a minute I was worried that she might be taking me to the headmistress's office. But instead we walked off the Miss Horton's campus and into town, where there was a tea parlor. Miss Ellison ordered English breakfast tea, and when I asked the waitress for a pot of Lapsang souchong tea—Grandmother's favorite—the waitress did a double take and said she'd never heard of it. So I settled for English breakfast too, and Miss Ellison sat back in her chair and looked at me for a long time.

Tell me about yourself, Julia, she said finally. I can tell that you've probably come from a very interesting background. You seem to know about such a huge array of unlikely things. I've taught at Miss Horton's for twenty years and I've never known another young woman like you.

She had a kind look on her face when she said this, so I knew she didn't mean it as an insult. I told her about growing up at Windy Ridge and my mother becoming a runaway hippie and how we went looking for her in our car and about everything that happened on the trip. At first Miss Ellison looked like she couldn't decide if I was making it all up, especially during the parts about the monkey at Tipsy Lipps's party and about the chicken foot and the voodoo houses in New Orleans. But by the time I got to World's End and then the part about Gold Point, she leaned forward in her chair and listened so hard, I don't even think that she remembered to blink her eyes. And then, when I told her what happened when we got to San Francisco and found my mother living on a mattress on a kitchen floor in a house filled with naked, dirty people, Miss Ellison put her hands over her mouth and stared at me in horror.

I got embarrassed then and stopped talking. Both of our pots of tea were empty and out of the corner of my eye, I could see that the waitress had been standing behind the counter listening to me too while she was pretending to wash cups.

When Miss Ellison was ready to talk again, she asked me: Why did your aunt bring you to Miss Horton's after all of this?

Because women in my family have been going to Miss Horton's for generations, I told her. And anyway, we left-over Lancasters don't have a home anymore. Aunt Constance said that she didn't know what else to do with me. She doesn't have a lot of money left, and Miss Horton's gave me a scholarship because I'm a Lancaster.

Miss Ellison didn't say anything.

And, I went on, Aunt Constance said I'd be safe here.

We walked slowly back to Miss Horton's. When we got back to the campus, I turned up the path to go back to my dorm room with the chalk line down the middle, but Miss Ellison made me follow her to the headmistress's office instead. I sat outside the office by myself while Miss Ellison and the headmistress had a long talk inside. Then they called me in when they were done.

Julia, said Miss Ellison. We think that for the rest of the semester, you should move out of your dorm room. I would like for you to come and live with me in my little house on the edge of campus.

Oh, I said warily. Why?

We just think you need a little extra attention, she told me. And frankly, I think you need a little kindness.

No, she corrected herself. A lot of kindness.

I didn't know what to say. It was quiet for a minute until Miss Ellison added:

If you need further convincing, you should know that I can play gin—and hearts and spades. Maybe not as well as your grandmother or Aunt Constance, but passably well. And I *have* always wanted to learn more about voodoo. So what do you say?

When I got back to my dorm room later that afternoon, I couldn't pack my bags fast enough.

CHAPTER THIRTEEN

A Fresh Pot of Tea

Miss Ellison had given me a nice room with white curtains and a window that looked into the branches of a tulip tree, which looked especially pretty when it was covered with winter snow and icicles. Miss Ellison also made very good banana bread and carrot cake, and she got my Brownie camera back from the headmistress and didn't seem to mind how many pictures I took. She even gave me a little mechanical bird in a cage to keep me company.

The cloud-over-sun feeling faded a little while I was living at Miss Ellison's, but I also didn't let myself get too comfy because I knew I couldn't stay there forever. I still didn't have a real home like all of the other girls here did.

On the last day of the semester, just before Christmas vacation, a lot of parents drove to Miss Horton's to pick up their daughters and take them home. Some parents just sent big black limousines driven by chauffeurs to pick them up. On the last day before vacation, one of the girls asked me during math class:

Is your boyfriend Sheriff Stone going to be sending a horse by to pick you up?

The other girls in the class snickered.

Aunt Constance came to get me instead. Our Windy

Ridge car looked very different when it didn't have trunks and silver candlesticks and carpets stuffed inside it and tied to the top. Aunt Constance had swapped out her summery straw hat and flowered dress for one of Grandmother's old fur hats and the mink coat we'd used as a blanket in the Texas desert.

Hello, Julia, she said as she hugged me into the front of the coat.

I breathed into the fur; it still smelled of Grandmother's perfume and I had such a pang for Windy Ridge that I almost cried. I was very happy to see Aunt Constance, but it was hard, too, because it was like having someone you love visit you in prison and knowing they eventually have to leave you there when they go back into the world again.

Miss Ellison served us banana bread in her living room, and at first she and Aunt Constance talked about the weather and the school endowment, whatever that was, and then of course the talk turned to the topic of me.

I'd like to say this delicately, said Miss Ellison, because I think Julia is a special girl. But it is precisely because she is so special and unusual that I bring it up. Have you considered educating her at home?

Aunt Constance looked very uncomfortable.

Well, at present, we are in between residences, she told Miss Ellison, and I knew that it embarrassed her to say so. Then she sat up very straight, and asked:

Is there some question about Julia's contribution to the Miss Horton's community?

Certainly not, said Miss Ellison. It's nothing like that. But I do not believe that Miss Horton's is the right place for your niece. She is misunderstood here.

What can you mean? asked Aunt Constance. She gave me a worried look. Has something happened? Are you all right, Julia?

Miss Ellison set down her plate.

Julia, do you mind making us a fresh pot of tea? she asked.

I wasn't fooled for a minute; I knew they just wanted to talk about me privately, but I got up and walked out of the room with a teapot anyway. Of course I stationed myself right on the other side of the door.

Miss Lancaster, I am afraid that six years at this school would destroy Julia's spirit, Miss Ellison told Aunt Constance. I understand that Julia's mother is absentee and that you are her de facto caretaker. I personally feel that she would be better off with you than in this very conventional environment. I would be happy to create a special Miss Horton's lesson plan for her and supervise her education from afar.

Aunt Constance was silent for a minute.

Miss Ellison, I'm sure that Julia is an unusual presence here at Miss Horton's, she said at last. But I'm not sure that I agree with you. I hardly know how to raise her. I don't have children of my own. I don't know that I'm . . . equipped to handle her.

But you *have* been raising her, said Miss Ellison. Julia has told me everything.

Yes, and since she's been in my care, she's learned how to shoot a gun and drive a car, said Aunt Constance. She has run away and taken money from my purse. All before she has even officially become a teenager. I'm afraid that she's running completely wild.

I honestly don't think that Julia is a rebel at heart, said Miss Ellison. I certainly think that she's high-spirited, but she's also very sweet. She has so much affection to share and no one to share it with.

She needs a mother, she added. Not necessarily her real mother. But someone who loves her and makes her feel safe.

I do love Julia, said Aunt Constance in a quavering

voice. And she's all that I have left. But don't you think she needs normalcy and to be around girls her own age? Especially after all that's happened?

I think that Julia needs love and understanding, and she's not getting enough of either thing here at Miss Horton's, said Miss Ellison. I can only do so much, but I promise to help you from here, Miss Lancaster. You and Julia will not be alone.

They were quiet for a minute, and then Miss Ellison called out:

Julia, how is that tea coming along?

I scrambled into the kitchen and made the fresh tea, and by the time I went back into the living room I could tell that something had been decided. Aunt Constance dabbed at her eyes with a handkerchief.

Julia, she said. We think that you should leave Miss Horton's and come live with me in the city. Miss Ellison would mail us your lessons and assignments, and we would mail them back to her to be graded. Is this agreeable to you?

I get to come live in a hotel with you again? I asked.

Yes, said Aunt Constance. Until I find us a permanent house.

But don't worry, she added. I still have all of our practical-travel things there, of course, to make us feel at home.

Miss Ellison helped us carry my things to the car.

Goodbye, Julia, she said as she hugged me. Merry Christmas to you both. Happy New Year too.

Just before she closed the car door, she leaned in and said:

I have a feeling that 1969 will be the year that you find home again.

Aunt Constance drove slowly down the snow-covered highway back toward New York City, and at first we were very quiet.

What are you thinking about, Julia? she asked me.

I was thinking about something that Madame Batilde said down in New Orleans, I told her.

I knew you were probably eavesdropping, said Aunt Constance. What part?

The part where she said that you'd find my real mother and that it wasn't Rosemary Lancaster, I said, and asked her: Do you think she meant that it was you?

Aunt Constance reached out and took my hand.

Maybe she did, she said. I'm going to do my best.

I've missed you, Julia, she added. It has been *very* lonely being the only Lancaster in town.

CHAPTER FOURTEEN

Out-of-the-Ordinary Happenings

Miss Ellison's mail-in lessons were hard. She asked me to write a lot of essays. A topic would arrive by letter, and I would sit and write each essay in a corner of the Barbizon Hotel lobby, where they'd set up a desk and a chair just for me:

One of the hardest topics: "What I Learned from My Trip Across America." I wrote almost ten long pages about all of the practical things I'd learned, such as:

1. *Catching a fish with my bare hands;*
2. *Setting up a sun tent from travel trunks and rugs;*
3. *Shooting a pistol;*
4. *Driving a car;*
5. *Excavating gold from a hill;*
6. *Outrunning a herd of wild javelina.*

But at the very end of the essay, I added:

I also learned that you probably shouldn't tell people (especially Miss Horton's girls) too much about trips like this, especially when very interesting, out-of-the-ordinary things have happened to you. Because not many people get to experience very interesting, out-of-the-ordinary things, and they don't believe that such things could happen to other people either. But out-of-the-ordinary things happen all the time, especially to Lancasters.

In fact, three more very interesting, out-of-the-ordinary things happened to Aunt Constance and me not long after I moved into the Barbizon Hotel with her:

OUT-OF-THE-ORDINARY HAPPENING #1

One cold February morning, while I was working on a Miss Ellison lesson and Aunt Constance sat nearby in a lobby chair reading the *New York Times* and drinking a cup of tea, she suddenly spat that tea back out into her cup. Some of it even came out of her nose, and the concierge rushed over to see if she was choking. She waved him away and said:

I'm fine, I'm fine, thank you, Rupert—

And then she went on reading something in the paper with her eyes very wide.

Julia, she said after a minute. It appears that—well—it appears that Shirley Hicks has passed away.

Who did what? I asked.

Shirley Hicks, said Aunt Constance. You recall—Tipsy von Lipp. She passed away. Died.

Oh, you mean Tipsy Lipps, I said. What happened?

The obituary says that she fell off a yacht while on holiday in Greece, said Aunt Constance. That poor, wretched woman. And it appears that Windy Ridge is going to be up for sale again, along with all of her other properties.

Can we try to buy it? I asked, sitting straight up.

Oh heavens, no, said Aunt Constance. We can't afford it anymore.

What about the money she gave us for Windy Ridge in the first place? I asked. Can't we just give it back?

We've been living on that money, Julia, said Aunt Constance. A lot of it's gone. So that's that. Windy Ridge will finally, truly go to strangers, with all of its ties to the Lancasters cut forever.

Then she went upstairs to our room and didn't come down again until the next morning.

Now it's time for me to talk about:

OUT-OF-THE-ORDINARY HAPPENING #2

Because my desk in the lobby of the Barbizon Hotel was so close to the revolving front door, every time someone came in or went out, a big whoosh of air would come in and blow my papers onto the floor. So I finally got fed up, marched upstairs, went through our travel trunks, and fished out my huge hunk of pyrite from Gold Point. I brought it back down to the lobby and plunked it on top of my papers.

And then, a few days after we found out about Tipsy Lipps falling off the yacht in Greece, I was sitting at my desk, minding my own business, when a woman with a big fox-fur stole and bright green eye shadow swept out of the hotel elevators and into the lobby. She glanced over at me and my desk as she marched toward the door. Then she stopped in her tracks and looked again.

Darlin', what is *that*? she asked me, pointing at the pyrite.

It's pyrite, I told her, and added: Also known as fool's gold. I found it in the Nevada hills last summer. And now it's my paperweight.

The woman leaned forward and squinted at it.

May I pick it up? she asked, and to my surprise, she

not only picked it up and turned it from side to side and felt its weight, she also sniffed it and then *licked* the side of it. I didn't know what to say. She put it back down very gently.

That ain't fool's gold, honey, the woman told me. That's the real deal. And I ought to know. My husband, Archibald Crest of Crest Minerals, Incorporated—rest his soul—mined half the gold out of South America. So if I were you, I'd cash that chunk in pronto and move into the Barbizon presidential suite.

Then she sailed out the revolving door.

It turns out that Archibald Crest's widow with the bright green eye shadow was right. I told Aunt Constance what she had said and that very afternoon we had the hunk appraised by a bank. It was real gold after all, every ounce of it. So the bank gave us a lot of money for it, which Aunt Constance put into a savings account, and I was going to have to find a new paperweight.

Now do we have enough to buy back Windy Ridge? I asked Aunt Constance in the taxi on the way home.

Aunt Constance smiled sadly and shook her head.

No, Julia, she said. Unfortunately not. But we have more than we did this morning, enough to keep us at the Barbizon for a good long time, and maybe buy a different house. We have to try to stop thinking about Windy Ridge. Let's count our other blessings instead.

That night before I went to sleep, I wrote Sheriff

Stone a letter and informed him that there was still real gold after all in Gold Point and told him exactly where I found my hunk, and said that I hoped there was more where it came from and that it would make him very rich. I also told him about my desk in the Barbizon lobby and about Tipsy Lipps's accident and how Windy Ridge was for sale again and a few other updates. Then I sealed the envelope and licked the stamp and mailed it off.

This now brings me to:

OUT-OF-THE-ORDINARY HAPPENING #3

About two months later, in April, the weather started to warm up, so Aunt Constance switched from her fur hat back to the straw one and we started to take walks in Central Park in the afternoons. Aunt Constance said that park walks were very healthy for the body and soul, and that in the old days, walking in the park was called promenading and ladies would carry frilly little umbrellas called parasols to protect their skin from the sun.

One afternoon we came back from our daily promenade and Gerald, who worked behind the Barbizon's front desk, said that a big envelope had arrived for me. I thought it was another lesson from Miss Ellison, but the postmark was from Nevada. I knew it must be from Sheriff Stone and ripped it open right away.

This is what his letter said:

Dear Deadeye,

Well you have no idea how happy I was to get your letter all those weeks ago, and sure enough, you were right and I was wrong. That isn't fool's gold in that hill at all, hallelujah. It's the yellow, the real deal, and there sure is plenty of it. I'm rich now, you bet, and I have you to thank for it.

And here in Gold Point, we find ways to thank our friends who do nice things for us. Look in this envelope to find a present from me, and please do come back to Gold Point as soon as you can. I'll have a pickax waiting for you, and you can take as much yellow back with you as you can carry in one of those old Lancaster travel trunks.

Your friend,
Sheriff Stone

I dug deep into the envelope like he told me to do and at the bottom was another piece of paper with a gold border, which looked very fancy and official. I handed it over to Aunt Constance and asked her what it was.

Suddenly she grasped her throat with her hand and I thought she might faint, but instead she exclaimed:

God in heaven. It's the deed to Windy Ridge. It looks

like Sheriff Stone has bought it for us. He put it in your name, Julia.

What does that mean? I asked her.

It means that you own Windy Ridge, cried Aunt Constance. That is, you'll get it when you're eighteen. Until then I'm your guardian.

She burst into tears.

We're going home, Julia. *Home.*

I wished that we had sparklers and firecrackers like the ones Belfry and I set off on Independence Day. The next best thing: to help us celebrate, the Barbizon concierge and the bellboys went into the hotel kitchen and came back out with a cake covered in candles, like it was our birthday instead of our home-going day:

Aunt Constance's face was filled with light. She got on the telephone and told a florist to send over a big passel of yellow roses for us to wear in our hair when we went to dinner. Then we ate at a gilded supper club wearing those roses, and Aunt Constance even let me have a half glass of champagne. There was a big band playing on a stage, and the bandleader noticed us sitting there happily at our table with our champagne; he came over and asked us what the occasion was. And when I told him what the occasion was, he said that he was dedicating the next song to us:

> *"Oh, you can go to the east,*
> *Go to the west,*
> *But someday you'll come*
> *Back where you started from."*

Aunt Constance and I got up and danced, and even though she only knew how to waltz and it was the wrong dance for the song, everyone in the room clapped anyway, and it was the best night of my whole life.

I just wished that Sheriff Stone could have been there. Something tells me that he would have liked dancing too.

EPILOGUE

I forgot how hot Windy Ridge summers were. But when we got there, Aunt Constance said that I was now old enough to go swimming in the Hudson River to cool off. Not the main part of the river, of course, with its fast currents, but in a new little side pool that swirled just at the bottom of the cliff stairs leading down from the house. The river had decided to make the side pool while Aunt Constance and I were driving across America looking for my mother.

It was nearly ninety degrees the day that Aunt Constance and I moved back home to Windy Ridge. The house was empty inside except for dust, and so we opened up every window and let the wind blow through the house to wake it up again after its yearlong sleep.

How does it feel to be back, Julia? said Aunt Constance.

It feels strange, I told her. But familiar too. Like being

in a dream where you're at your house, but everything is just a little different than it is in real life.

It's not quite the same, I agree, said Aunt Constance. But that's all right. You and I are different now after all that's happened. Why shouldn't Windy Ridge be different too?

It still feels wonderful to be back, though, she said softly, and wandered off into the living room, running her hands along the walls, which were empty except for the marks where Lancaster paintings and portraits had once hung.

Later that day, we spread one of the Oriental carpets from our stash of practical-travel things on one of the back lawns and sat on it and looked out across the grounds. Everything was very overgrown and brambly and wild. That was another way that Windy Ridge had decided to change while we were gone.

I like it this way, I told Aunt Constance.

So do I, she said. We'll keep it wild. It's a new era here at Windy Ridge.

Just then we heard the faint sound of the doorbell ringing inside the house.

I'll go, I told Aunt Constance, and I ran up the stone stairs to the slate-floored back terrace and into the house, through the main hallway where the grandfather clock used to stand. The front door had swollen in its frame and I had to pull hard with my whole body weight to get it open.

There on the other side stood Belfry, holding a small cardboard box.

Hi, I said.

Hi, he said back.

We stood there for a minute, staring at each other. He looked taller and older and had a fresh haircut. He smelled minty, like he'd just brushed his teeth, and suddenly I wondered how I looked to him. Pretty, I hoped. Even though I knew from the tarot cards that I wasn't going to marry him someday.

Did you get all of my postcards? I asked him.

Belfry reached into his back pocket and pulled out a stack of them.

You sure went to a lot of places, he said. Around the whole world, it seemed like.

We were quiet again until I remembered my Lancaster manners and asked him to come in out of the sun.

It sure looks different in here without all of the Lancaster stuff, he said as we walked through the house, and he added: Are you going to get it back?

We can't, I said. It's all sold. But we still have a few things from before. Our practical-travel things. Aunt Constance says it's all we need these days.

Belfry looked down at the postcards I'd sent him.

Aren't you going to be bored being back here after going to all of these places? he asked.

Maybe someday, I told him. But it's so different now

that it's kind of like being on another adventure. It's a new home and an old home all at once.

The wind blew through the house, and we could smell lilac on the breeze. That is what summer smelled like at Windy Ridge. Lilac and cut grass and thunderstorm rain and baked heat rising out of the terrace slate at sundown.

I brought you a welcome-home present, said Belfry, and he gave me the cardboard box. Inside was the china teacup that we'd filled with dirt and tobacco seeds last summer, the day before Grandmother died. The dirt was still inside it.

Did the tobacco ever grow? I asked him.

Nope, he said. But maybe it will now that you're back.

We put the cup on a windowsill and walked outside to join Aunt Constance in the garden. The three of us sat there together, watching the bees in the grass and the leaves blowing in the river breeze—and I swear that not a single cloud crossed in front of the sun all day.

The End

ACKNOWLEDGMENTS

The author wishes to thank Erin Clarke, Molly Friedrich, Lucy Carson, Jay Mandel, Gregory Macek, Glynnis MacNicol, Sally Quinn, Sue Fry, Victoria Wasserman, Liesl Schillinger, and Stephan Wurth for their invaluable contributions to this book and the experiences that inspired it.

ACKNOWLEDGMENTS

ABOUT THE AUTHOR

Lesley M. M. Blume is an author and journalist. She lives in New York City but is a nomad at heart. When she travels the world, she always takes with her a trunk filled with glistening practical-travel things. She has written five previous novels for Knopf, including *Cornelia and the Audacious Escapades of the Somerset Sisters* and *Tennyson,* which the *Chicago Tribune* praised for its "brilliant, unusual writing."